Black Fawn Academy

Black Fawn Academy

by
KIRK MENAPACE

1

Nightmare

"DARKNESS—WE experience it many times before, during, and after our lives. It can be both peaceful and scary, calming and unnerving. Some of us grew up with a fear of the dark and the unknown monsters and evil that could be hiding in it. But as we got older, we learned that's just not how things work. However, that is the catch: you don't really know what anything is about until you are enlightened. After all, what would be the point of knowing everything from the start? Would life even be an adventure without the suspense, fear, and chaos that it brings?" The documentary stated as it was quickly drowned out by my father.

"Oh crap," my father said. "I just spilled my drink all over my shirt. I'll be back in a second."

He set the glass down and walked by me and ruffled my hair with his hands. I sat there looking at the dog lying by the fireplace and the snow coming down outside. *I am so glad I am not out there right now*, I thought to myself. The fire was brightening the room and flashing off the maroon-colored walls. Then I saw Slider perk his head up out of his deep slumber. He looked at me then the window, and his fur stood up on his back. He began to growl and got up and approached the window.

"Help…"

I heard a faint scream from the distance beyond the walls of our home. I got up out of my chair to look at what Slider was staring at. There was a woman: she was walking toward our home in the midst of this blizzard outside. I told Slider to lie down, and I put my jacket and boots on and started for the door.

"Where are you going?" my dad grunted, walking into the room.

He was a tall and muscularly built man. He had a short beard coming in dark brown. His hair was falling out, but you could tell he cared about it because he refused to shave it off.

"There's a woman outside! She needs help," I said to him quickly.

I grabbed the doorknob and opened the door; the brisk air froze my hair on my face and in my nose. It was around –10 degrees Fahrenheit right now. I spotted the woman about forty yards or so from the house, so I ran to her and helped her through the snow back to our house. She seemed to be slightly underdressed for the weather, wearing just a winter jacket and pants. She did not have snow boots or gloves or a hat on. She had long red hair and eyes like sapphires. She had an athletic build to her but still wholesome.

"Thank you," she muttered under her breath as I helped her down next to the fire.

"Seems a little late for a hike in the wilderness, isn't it, miss?" my dad said to her.

"Why yes, it is. I'm so lucky I found a place to find shelter. My car has broken down on the road about a mile or so from your house. I figured it was best to find help rather than wait and freeze in my car," she said shyly.

"Well, you are safe now, sweetie," Father said warmly to her. "Andrew, go grab the woman something to drink and eat."

I took my leave and headed for the kitchen. I heard my father and the woman talking in the other room as I was fetching a glass of water and some leftover stew on the stove for our guest. After a couple minutes, I made my way back to the room, which was awkwardly quiet. I set the food and water down on the table in front of the young woman.

"Thank you," she said quietly.

"Oh no, are you okay?" I asked her.

She had blood on her hands; I must have not noticed that when I was helping her inside originally.

"Oh yes, I'm fine. That's not my blood, sweetie," she said calmly, looking up at me.

I turned to my father and my heart sank. There was a knife sticking out of his chest where his heart was. His head was tilted back on the chair and staring blankly at the ceiling.

"But...but...why...why...would you do this?" I said, panicked, turning back toward her.

But it was too late: I felt sudden pain in my gut and the warmth that followed.

"This is why I carry two," she said softly to me as she twisted the knife.

"You really shouldn't let your guard down," she said, and she let go of the knife and let me fall to my knees.

"Enjoy your movie. I'm sorry I cut it short," she said with a smile on her face as she opened the door and left the house.

She closed the door behind her, and I was left kneeling there, staring at the knife in me. *I need to call for some help*, I thought to myself, but I was becoming light-headed and weak from the injury. Then…darkness.

2
The Big Day

I ROSE FROM my bed drenched in sweat. *Just a nightmare*, I thought to myself as I looked out the window. It was a warm summer morning on the tropical island that I found myself so luckily living on.

"Andrew, get up, you lazy bum!" I heard my father yell from downstairs.

I made my bed and threw a shirt on from the ground that I had worn from the past couple days. Black—that was the mandatory color for our school. I put on my pants and did my morning hygiene. I came downstairs and saw my dad standing in the kitchen, drinking his coffee.

"It's going to be a warm one today, son," he said glancing quickly at his watch. "I'm going to be late for work, so I need to head out. Make sure you lock the door on your way out!" He slipped his gun into his waistband and headed out to his truck.

More of a tank, it would seem, seeing as it was completely

up-armored to keep him well protected on his drive. *I hate school*, I thought to myself as I quickly ate my cereal at the table. I finished and put the bowl in the sink and made my way out of the house and to my car. As I was getting in, I glanced at the tree line and could have sworn I saw someone staring at me. I get that feeling sometimes, like someone is watching me or just a presence existing behind me. I got in my car and drove to school within reasonable time. I parked my car in the back lot, so I did not have to talk to anyone on the way into the building, which was three stories tall with multiple guard towers surrounding the facility. There was a barbed-wire fence that ran around the compound for "protection"—at least that is what the guards always have said.

"Hey, Andy," I heard a girl's voice from behind me.

"Oh, hey, Anya," I said, turning around.

God, she is pretty, I thought to myself. She had black hair pulled back into a bun without a hair out of place. With hazel eyes and rather long eyelashes, she was about my height, which was exceedingly tall for a girl.

"You ready for the big test today?" Anya said happily.

"How can you be so excited about a test?" I groaned. "You are such a nerd."

"I just find this all so exhilarating," she said, clasping her hands near her face.

"Yeah, yeah, let's get inside then, shall we?" I said, walking toward the entrance.

"Morning," the guard said firmly as we entered the building.

"Good day, sir," I said as I scanned my hand on the terminal.

I saw the green light pop up, and I walked through the detector.

"Why would we want to sneak any weapons in here?" I said sarcastically to the guard.

"Oh, you know the drill, Andrew. Good luck on your test today."

"Thanks!" I yelled back as I was rounding the corner with Anya.

"I've been training my whole life for this moment, Andrew," Anya said excitedly as we approached the elevator.

"I'm aware, you are just a big ole nerd," I said jokingly.

We got on the elevator and pressed the ground-floor button for five seconds. The door closed, and then the wall behind us opened. We entered the next room and scanned our retinas before the door clicked to unlock and let us in.

"Andy, Anya, what's up, you guys!" we heard from inside the room.

The class was full of students standing around each other's desks talking. At the front of the classroom, there were two tables, and I saw some items on them but could not tell what they were from this far away.

"Not much, Igor, just ready to get this show on the road." I said, giving him a cool handshake we had come up with.

Igor and Anya had both been my friends since I was a child. Igor was a tall, brutish-looking guy. He had blonde hair and blue eyes. He had a massive tattoo that looked like it was growing up the side of his arm. Poorly done, but still you could tell he did it to show how cool he was rather than for the art itself.

"It's crazy that we have already spent eight years here at

Black Fawn Academy and we are already getting ready for the big test," Igor said with his eyes flashing fire.

"You both are killing me with this enthusiasm," I said, looking between the two of them.

"Everyone, take your seats!" yelled Professor Aminoff.

We all sat in our assigned seats quickly not to irritate Aminoff. He was a very strict and eccentric man. He had white hair all over the place, and his tie was always messed up and his shirt slightly untucked. His pistol was always so immaculate, though. He kept that thing in mint condition.

"Today's the big day," he said, staring at all of us. "I'm happy that I got the chance to train you guys over the years. You are an exceptional lot. Before we begin, I want everyone to remember that you have been trained to be the best of the best. Whether you pass or fail, just know I appreciate each and every one of you and know that you will move on to do great things after graduation. Are there any questions before we begin?" Professor Aminoff's eyes darted across the room to make sure no hands had popped up.

"All right, then, Dimitri and Anya, you two are up first."

"Good luck," I told her as she walked toward the front of the room.

Dimitri and Anya stood across from one another in the front of the class. They both approached their respective tables and seemed to be choosing an item.

"Just one weapon," I heard Aminoff say softly to Anya.

"I don't need a weapon to fight a girl," Dimitri said, chuckling.

He was about average height for a high schooler. Hair was

slicked back and very dark. He had on a black polo shirt and black slacks that seemed to have a hole toward the bottom.

"Ha, you'll regret that choice shortly," Anya said under her breath.

"Begin!" yelled the professor.

Like lightning, Anya darted across the room to Dimitri. Through the process she had drawn her knife forward and was lunging rather quickly for his chest. Dimitri blocked by swiftly grabbing her wrist and snapping it back, dropping the knife from her hand.

"Argh," Anya grunted as the knife hit the floor.

She swept her leg toward him, knocking him off-balance and freeing herself from his grasp. She went for the knife, but Dimitri kicked her right in the nose, knocking her on her back. Blood was running down her face as she looked at Dimitri, who began to get up. He picked up the knife and stood over her body.

"As I said earlier, I don't need a weapon to fight a girl. But since you brought me one, I might as well use it." He brought the knife down onto her neck, but she stopped the blade with her hand.

"Shame you would think I'd go down this easy," Anya said.

She clicked her heels on the ground, and two blades sprung out of the toes of her boots. She drove the left leg up into the inner thigh of Dimitri, severing the femoral artery in his leg. He fell to one knee, still trying to force the knife into Anya's body. She then brought her right foot up to his left rib, puncturing his chest cavity and causing a sucking chest wound. Dimitri let go of the knife and fell to his side. Gasping for air, he lay there staring at the rest of us as the life faded from his eyes. Anya got up slowly and looked down at Dimitri.

"Not going to lie," she said, winded, "I really did think I was going to go down that easy."

The class applauded her, and Professor Aminoff came to her grinning. "Congratulations, Anya. Go ahead and take yourself to medical to take care of your injuries."

"Yes, sir," she said and headed for the door.

"Good luck, you two," Anya said to Igor and me.

"Hey, Andrew," Igor said.

"Yeah, what's up man?" I asked.

He sounded concerned for a second.

"There's something I've been wanting to tell…" He was cut short as Professor Aminoff yelled,

"Igor and Andrew, you two are next. Get up here."

We looked at one another and made our way to the front of the room. *Shame*, I thought to myself. *Why would I be paired up with my best friend for my final test?* The whole situation seemed completely unfortunate, especially since Igor was so much more muscular than I. Then I remembered that strange nightmare that I'd had last night.

"Get ready," Aminoff said, as I was trying to decide what weapon to choose.

However, I noticed Igor was not selecting a weapon, just standing there, shoulders slouched, staring at me.

"Begin!" Aminoff yelled.

I could have sworn Igor would have charged me with his brute strength. Since he decided not to pick a weapon, I saw no physical threat being presented by him, which was, again, strange. I lunged quickly across the room toward him, closing the distance. As I made it to him, I leapt and grabbed the collar of his shirt. While in the air, I crossed my arms from one another and flung Igor to the ground. I gained the dominant position over him as I held the choke. I watched as my best friend died before my eyes by my own hands. When it was over, I realized that he had not even tried to defend himself. *What had he been trying to tell me before the test?* I thought to myself.

"Well, that was anticlimactic," sighed the professor. "Oh well, a passing grade is a passing grade. Go have a wait in the next room, Andrew."

"Will do, Professor," I said as I approached the door to the next room.

3
Mind Games

AS I ENTERED the room, I noticed a table, a machine with some wires, two chairs, and a mirror, which seemed to be fogged up and smudged along the wall. From my experience I realized that I made it to the interrogation phase of my test. The mirror was clearly double-sided, and no doubt Professor Aminoff was on the other side grading how I did. My eyes drifted around the room to notice every inch of it, to have it in my memory, every crack, every smudge on the floor, and anything that could possibly seem out of place in this sort of situation. I sat down in the chair facing the mirror and had the table with the machine on my left side.

Click.

The door unlocked behind me, and a man walked in rather briskly.

"Don't turn around," he said to me firmly as he approached the table. "Do you know why we are here, young man?"

"Yes," I said blankly, still looking at his distorted figure in the mirror in front of me.

"Good, I'll get you hooked up and we will begin," he said as he began hooking the wires up to the machine and his laptop to the back.

He peeled back the plastic and stuck the wires to separate parts of my body. The wires were attached to a sticky, bluish gel. A polygraph—I'd figured as much.

"Are you nervous?" the man said.

"Only people who have something to hide would be nervous about something like this," I said gently, still staring straight-ahead, avoiding eye contact.

He sat down behind the table, and then we began.

"Please state your name for the record," he said sternly.

"Andrew Franco Bertolini," I said back to him.

"Mr. Bertolini, have you ever heard of a man named Igor Rustovar?"

"I have."

"And how did you know Mr. Rustovar?" he asked.

"We grew up together and were close friends."

"Did you see him today?"

"Yes."

"Did you murder him?"

"No."

"Do you happen to know who could have possibly murdered Mr. Rustovar or their intentions in doing so?"

"No, but he will be missed. He was a very close friend, if not a brother to me," I said calmly, still looking at the mirror.

"Have you ever heard of a black site named Black Fawn Academy?"

"Never heard of it," I said.

"Interesting. Well, maybe if I talk about it, it could jog your memory?" he said, sounding intrigued by my response. "Black Fawn Academy is a school that takes children at a young age and trains them to be field operatives. They learn everything from assassination techniques, poisons, survival, methods of torture, interrogation, building false identities, and feeling no remorse, nothing except for the gratification of completing whatever mission is presented to them. They align themselves with no specific country or government. They simply do as they are told and make the Black Fawn absurd amounts of money."

"Sounds all very interesting. But as I said before, I've never heard of it. Sorry. I'm just a typical high school student."

"Do you have a family?" he asked.

"Just my father and my dog Slider," I said, still in the same monotone voice, trying not to change the pitch of my voice with my answers.

"What does your father do for work?" he said.

"He's the principal at my high school," I stated.

"Would you say you know him well?" he asked curiously.

"I mean, he is my father, so I'd hope so," I said sarcastically.

I do not think he liked that too much, because I heard a sneer from him after that remark.

"So you are telling me you've never heard of Black Fawn Academy. Your best friend whom you just saw today was killed and you know nothing about it, and you are just an average high school student?"

"Yes," I said sharply.

"You are lying," The man said as he slammed his fist onto the table angrily. "You are going to tell me the truth."

He was coming around the corner of the table and approaching me directly now. He had a scar coming down the front of his face. You could tell he never missed a day in the gym. He also smelled like he had not showered in weeks.

"I can make things rather…uncomfortable," he said, grinning.

He pulled a pair of pliers from his pocket and grabbed ahold of my hand. He had the craziest look in his eye, but I dare not break my role in all of this.

"Whatever you are planning on doing with those, it won't change my answer."

He placed the pliers under one of my fingernails and sighed. "They always choose the hard way," he grumbled.

Pulling upward and swiftly, he removed the nail from my finger. I flinched slightly but held my mouth shut and refused to make a noise.

"Tough guy, eh?" he said as he moved the pliers to another finger. "Well, I have all day, and we still have the toes to go after these fingers," he said through a laugh.

"That's enough, Richard," a mechanical voice said, coming from the mirror in front of me. "Mr. Bertolini, I'm not surprised you did well."

A light flipped behind the mirror, and I saw Professor Aminoff and my father standing behind it.

"Obviously an interrogation would be a lot longer than

this," my father said bluntly. "However, for schoolhouse purposes that's all we needed."

"Yes, as unfortunate as it is that you had to kill your best friend, it was necessary as a final step to see how well you can control your emotions and lie under pressure." Aminoff paused for a moment and seemed to be rubbing his fingers together. "Eventually, you forget who you used to be." He continued staring at the ground now.

"That's enough now, Aminoff. Don't be scaring him on his big day."

"Right, well, congratulations, Mr. Bertolini. You are officially on the list for graduation," said the professor. "We will discuss your first mission once we complete the graduation ceremony. Until then, go ahead and rest up and celebrate. I'm sure your father wants to enjoy some time with you before you leave the island."

4

Graduation

"I'M PROUD of you, son," my father said to me as we were leaving the schoolhouse. "If your mom were still here, I know she'd feel the same way."

He grabbed my shoulder and pulled me in and gave me a tight squeeze.

"Seems you do have some emotions after all," I said, trying not to suffocate in his arms.

I instantly felt my balance leaving me as he knocked me to the ground.

"Never let your guard down," he said, smirking as he extended his hand to help me back up.

I gave a chuckle because I should have anticipated that coming. My father was a very cold man, but he was so out of love. We do not have a traditional family, but in order to survive this lifestyle, you must learn to control your emotions. We simply do not get to enjoy the luxuries of talking about our feelings. Heck, while other kids were playing baseball, my dad was teaching me how to properly get rid of a dead body.

"You want to do anything special for dinner tonight?" my father said.

"No, really it's not that big of a deal. I'm just finally becoming an adult, right?" I said, looking up at him.

"Of course, more than you realize," he said. "Well, I'll tell you about my graduation exam when we get home, over some dinner. I'll meet you at home. Be there in about thirty minutes and don't be late," he said, looking down at his watch again.

He must have had a meeting he forgot about because he seemed to be in a rush when he walked away from me. My vision then went dark, and I felt cold around my eyes. Hands— someone's hands were covering my eyes.

"Guess who," I heard a muffled voice say from behind.

It was obviously a girl pretending to sound like a grown man. "I'm surprised you passed an exam with an awful voice like tha—" But before I could finish, she flung me around and had me by my collar.

"Your dad is right; you are letting your guard down today." Anya snorted.

My face must have turned red from this comment because she immediately began making fun of me. *Girls are so annoying*, I thought to myself.

"Look, Anya, I have some things I need to do at home. I can't hang out right now."

"That's okay," she said. "Have you seen Igor? We were going to celebrate together after the exam since his parents are out on mission."

"I don't think that's going to happen, Anya," I said quietly looking toward the ground. I raised my head and made direct eye contact with her.

"I was put up against him for the final test while you were in medical."

"No…that can't be."

"Unfortunately, it is the truth," I said to her. "I'm sorry, but I was just following protocol."

She looked back at me as if peering into my soul.

"I understand, Andrew, you don't have to explain. This is our job, and we do what the mission requires," she said coldly.

We both stood there for a moment, and we felt the warm island breeze between our paths.

"Well, then, I should be going," she said as she walked toward her car in an uncertain manner.

"You liked him…didn't you?" I asked.

She stopped for a moment and then turned around, and I saw a tear rolling down her face. "He was everything I wanted." She turned back around and continued to her car. She got in, and I waved to her as she drove away.

I took a moment and admired the weather that we were having today on the island. Crazy to think that there would be such a place so far and secretive from the rest of civilization. I walked back to my car to get in and noticed something was stuck on the side of it. *A zip tie?* I thought to myself as I reached for it. Suddenly I felt a yank from my shirt as I was pulled into a van. I felt a slight poke in my arm as I was being dragged into the back. I saw three men with guns all pointed at me. There was also a man in the passenger seat who didn't make an effort to turn around to see what was going on.

"Don't speak, and just listen," one of them said.

They were wearing all black and had masks on that looked like deer heads with decent-sized antlers.

"Tonight, when you get home, you will put this in your fathers drink." He handed me a small vial with a clear liquid inside of it.

I looked at them, puzzled, but assumed it was some sort of poison. They then opened the door of the van and just let me crawl out like nothing happened. I opened my door and started up the engine to the car. The van pulled away out of the parking lot behind me. I drove back home, trying to consider who possibly just grabbed me out of the parking lot. Maybe this was my first mission? No, that could not be. My father would have warned me about something like this. I pulled into the driveway and was looking at my house when I got that same feeling I had this morning. *Someone is watching me*. I looked at the tree line and saw no one, but I could not shake the feeling. I got out of my car and approached my house but did not hear any barking. Usually, Slider would have come running to the door by now to greet me or let me know he was okay. I opened the door and still did not see him anywhere.

"Slider?" I said curiously as I shut the front door behind me.

Nothing, absolute quiet. *Strange*, I thought to myself, *where could he possibly be?* I went to the living room and saw him sleeping next to the window, bathing in the sunlight. I gave his head a pat and said,

"Do you do anything else all day?"

But he did not move. His breathing seemed to be normal, and there were no signs that he was hurt.

"Slider?" I said this time poking his nose to see if I could get some reaction from him. *Maybe If I get a treat, he will wake up*, I thought to myself as I went to the kitchen. But as I entered, I noticed something strange: the blinds by the sliding glass door were moving. The door was open, and the gentle breeze was making them dance before my eyes. I walked over to shut the door; I peeked my head outside to give a quick glance. No footprints, no evidence of the lock being picked or broken. *Whatever*, I thought to myself as I came back inside. By this point Slider was walking into the kitchen wagging his tail.

"You lazy turd," I said to him as I patted his head and scratched his belly.

I washed my hands and began preparations for dinner. I laid out all the produce on the counter and began sharpening my knife when the front door opened.

"Well, that didn't take long," I said, as my father walked into the kitchen.

"I know, right? No one showed up to the meeting."

"That's very unorthodox for the council," I said to him as he was looking at the food I was preparing.

"What are you making?" he said with his brow furrowed.

"Broccoli cheese casserole and steak."

"Awesome, I'm going to go change. I'll be down in a second." He headed for the stairs and made his ascent to the second floor.

I finished prepping the food and put the casserole in the

oven. *The vial*, I thought to myself as I closed the oven door. I prepared two drinks and poured the liquid from the vial I'd been given into one of the cups. I took them over to the table and got the table ready for dinner.

"I'll grill the steaks," my father said as he entered the room.

"Sounds good," I said as he grabbed the plate of steaks and headed for the sliding glass doors.

"Medium rare?" he asked.

"Still mooing," I said as he shut the door.

I went upstairs to change my clothing and get ready for the evening. As I came back down, my father was bringing the steaks in and placing one on each of our plates. The timer dinged, and I pulled the casserole out of the oven. I placed it on the center of the table so that we could both easily reach it. We sat down and said grace, and then began serving our food.

"Well, I told you I'd tell you about my graduation test," he said, taking a sip of his drink. "My brother..."

"What?" I asked. "You have a brother?"

"I had a brother," he said, cutting into his steak.

"You had to kill your own brother for your graduation test?" I was astonished.

"Yes, I never knew my mother or father. My brother and I were found at an orphanage at a young age and brought to the island as some of the first students to attend Black Fawn Academy. I did not become the principal overnight." He chuckled. "Anyways, yes, I had to kill my brother for my test. So I can understand the pain you are feeling deep down. Unlike you, I had no friends growing up or even in the academy. So the only person I would truly feel pain about losing was my own kin and the only person in my life at the time," he said as he coughed.

He seemed to begin to sweat as well. Something did not seem right about him. Maybe it was whatever I so willingly put in his drink.

"Anyways, there's a reason why I'm telling you this, son. I've been thinking a lot lately, and the meeting I had earlier was supposed to discuss who will take my place as principal of the academy."

"You are retiring?" I asked, uncertain of why he would do this.

"No, that's not it, I really need to…" His sentence was cut short as he began having a coughing fit.

He looked at me and then quickly realized what was going on.

"You…You…" he said in between coughs.

He fell from his chair and was lying still. I got out of my chair and rushed over to him.

"Father?" I said as I was shaking him.

"Shame." I jumped as I heard this voice coming from the other room.

"Good evening, Andrew," I heard as Professor Aminoff walked into the room.

"Professor?" I asked. "What's going on here?"

"The council decided your father must die."

Not only had I killed my best friend today but also my own father? My head was swelling with confusion; I had so many questions.

"He was a great mentor," Aminoff began, "but he began to search for something…he should have left hidden."

"Why me? Why have me do it out of all people?" I said, looking down at my father.

"The same reason that we had you kill young Igor."

"What?" I asked confused.

"Did Igor try to tell you anything important this morning on your way into class today?"

I had almost forgotten. He had said there was something important that he needed to tell me.

"Well, unfortunately Igor happened to be eavesdropping the other night when we discussed taking care of your father as well as the plan to do so."

"You had me kill him so I wouldn't figure out," I said, looking sharply at the professor now.

"Yes, that is exactly right. But you are looking at this the wrong way, Mr. Bertolini. You have so much in store for you, and you have accomplished so much already."

Argh...I felt a sudden pain in my stomach as I fell to my knees.

"Oh yes, you will start your mission immediately. After you wake up, of course. I had to drug you earlier in the van," he said, grinning at me.

That is right, I felt a poke earlier when I was snatched up. It must have been some slow-acting sleeping medication. "Anyways, get some rest," he said, standing over me. "When you wake up, you'll be right where you need to be."

Then I passed out.

5

The Sanctuary

"THIS ONE sure does sleep a while," a man said.

I opened my eyes, and I saw two people standing at the edge of a bed I was lying in.

"Where…where am I?" I asked them.

I looked around the room, and it seemed the walls were made from concrete and the floor as well. There were several other beds in the room and a couple of metal lockers lined along the back wall on either side of the door.

"The Sanctuary, of course," the man said.

"Well, one of them, that is," said the woman right after.

"Who are you two?" I asked as I began to sit up in the bed. *My head is absolutely killing me right now.*

"We are recruits just like you," said the woman. "My name's Katie."

"And I'm Kevin," said the man.

They seemed to be in complete sync; these two must have

known each other for a while. They both were wearing all-black uniforms as tradition of the organization. Kevin was tall, at least six feet or so, and surprisingly skinny. He had jet-black hair and brown eyes. I would be surprised if he had any physical strength at all. I would also assume the poison realm is more of his style. Katie was the opposite: she was shorter and had blue hair but still had brown eyes. She was extremely muscular—I was honestly surprised she didn't tell me her name was Helga.

"Blue…isn't very inconspicuous," I blurted out.

At that point Kevin giggled and then immediately stopped when Katie gave him a very draconic look.

"I didn't mean to offend you," I said to make sure I did not just insult my new family.

"When you stack bodies like I do, it doesn't matter what color your hair is," she said rather coldly.

Great, I was rather bad with social interactions, one of the main reasons why I hated going to school every day. I found myself more natural in a secluded area.

"Anyways, put your shoes on. We should be heading to dinner," Kevin said as he slapped my back.

I saw a pair of shoes lying underneath the foot of my bed, positioned perfectly with the toes of the shoe at equal length of the foot board. Strange, as I was putting them on, I noticed some very odd things about the rest of the room. For example, all the beds were made the same way, the lamps were positioned on the nightstands dead center. All the wall lockers were perfectly spaced out from one another. I finished tying my laces and stood up.

"Right, then, where are we eating?" I asked.

I was pretty hungry and felt like I'd been asleep for ages.

"The mess hall, of course. Did your school tell you nothing about your first assignment?"

"No," I said, confused.

Which made Kevin and Katie now both equally confused. We began walking through the corridor. The ceilings were very low, almost like we were in a bunker.

"Wait, you two didn't graduate from Black Fawn Academy?" I asked.

"Negative, I graduated from Crimson Hand Academy," said Katie.

"I graduated from Gold Thorn Academy," said Kevin.

I had never heard of either of those places. I did not even know that there was more than one academy to begin with. I really should have paid more attention to the global intelligence class I took. We stopped suddenly, and Katie pointed at a door.

"This is the common area; we usually gather in here after missions to relax. On the other side of the corridor are the latrines," she said as we continued down the corridor to a set of double doors.

They seemed to be solid oak with very rusted iron handles on them. She pulled the door open, and it gave light to a dining area with a harvest table. There was a chandelier above the table lit with candles. There was also magnificent art that looked like da Vinci hanging on the walls.

"How many people live here?" I asked, perplexed by how many seats there were.

"Yeah, about that...since the last inquisition we seemed to have...dwindled in numbers," Kevin said shyly.

"Ssseven." I heard a whisper from behind me that was rather chilling and unexpected. I turned around quickly to see a very pale-looking man. His black hair completely covered up his right eye, but the eye I could see was green. He was not wearing black pants and a tactical shirt like the rest of us. Rather, he was in a black robe with a red rope around his waist. His face was inches from me, and he was uncomfortably close. I took a small step back.

"Hello, you must be the janitor," I said jokingly, trying to emphasize that he was dressed weirdly compared to us.

"No, I'm tttthe torturer," he said rather grumpily.

Kevin was still giggling at the janitor comment but stopped when Katie punched his arm.

"Tttthe name is Ssssal."

"Nice to meet you, Sal," I said as I stuck out my hand.

He looked down at my hand rather nervously. He then slowly backed away into the shadows of the corridor and disappeared.

"He is an odd one," I said to Katie and Kevin.

"Yes, and a rather vindictive human, so please do not joke with him," Katie said.

"So he said seven of us. Where are the other three?" I asked, looking around in the dining area.

"The other three are Raven, who is our Scout; George, who is in charge of the demolition for when things get…iffy; and the leader, Dragutin, who is currently with them," stated Kevin. "They just went out on a mission recently and should be back later tonight or early in the morning."

"Great," I said as we sat down at the table to eat.

I was absolutely starving at this point. We were having salmon with mashed potatoes, garlic bread, and a wonderful-looking salad.

"Who made all of this?" I asked.

"Oh yes, there aren't really seven of us. We also have chefs who are contracted to us," said Katie.

This food was amazing. To think that I wouldn't have to cook or do the dishes again—what a heartwarming thought.

"So, uh, Black Fawn Academy, huh?" Kevin said.

"Yes, I started school there when I was ten. The first part of my life I still spent on the island, just at an actual school. Black Fawn didn't want us to be incompetent," I said, taking a bite of the creamy mashed potatoes.

"Oh yes, we know all about it. That is one of the most prestigious school to get into. I don't think I've actually met someone from there yet," Kevin said. "For example, I came from Gold Thorn Academy. My schooling was taught on the practice of pharmacology. Which is why I am here at the Sanctuary."

"And I was taught nothing but pain and destruction since I was a child," said Katie. "The Crimson Hand Academy taught us nothing but physical ways to assassinate as well as how to adapt and overcome any potential field risk."

Strange, I thought. *I learned how to do both of those at my school. I did not realize how well-rounded I am apparently.*

"You must be in line to take Dragutin's spot," Katie said, looking at me like I was some sort of idol.

"I only just arrived here, how would I be made leader of the Sanctuary?" I asked, confused.

"He would take you in as an apprentice," I heard from the doorway as a man entered the room. He was very muscular and had brown hair and brown eyes. He had a rather bushy mustache hanging over either side of his mouth.

"Master Dragutin of the Western Sanctuary at your service," he said, sticking out his hand. "Your father was one amazing operative."

"You knew my father?" I asked him.

"Why, of course, he helped me start a war. After that incident I was awarded the spot as master of this sanctuary years and years ago," he said excitedly. "It's great to have someone with experience and knowledge passed down from a man like him. You'll do well here, and I look forward to working alongside you."

"Me as well, sir," I said to him.

I had so many questions tumbling through my head right now.

"I'm afraid I have to send a report to HQ. Enjoy your meal, everyone," Dragutin said as he left the room.

I saw a rather slender and short woman standing in the doorway. She was peering in at us from the shadows.

"Don't be shy, Raven. Andrew is really cool," said Katie. Raven entered the room. I would be surprised if she cleared being five feet tall. She had blond hair and blue eyes, and she was staring at me and blushing.

"H-Hi, Andy. I'm Raven. It's a pleasure to meet you," she said as she sat down next to me.

"We were just telling Andrew about the academies we came from before you showed up," said Kevin.

"Oh! I'm from Falcon's Reach Academy. I learned all about

scouting and gathering intelligence," she said, smiling at me and preparing her food.

"And I am from the one and only Cannon Ridge Academy!" I heard a man yell as he walked into the room assertively.

He was of average height and build with no hair and brown eyes. When he looked at me, I noticed his left eye was a fake.

"Bit of a learning curve," he said. He must have noticed me looking at the eye. "I did it as a child. Note to self: Never put your face too close to the combustible material. No matter how small," he added, leaning in very close to me.

"Give the man some room, George," Katie said.

"Of course!" he bellowed as he walked around the table and took his seat to eat with us as well.

We all exchanged casual conversation about childhood memories of our schools, the good and the bad, as we finished up our meals.

"Well, we should probably turn in for the night," George said as he stood up from the table.

"It was so good to finally meet you," Raven said to me as they both left the room.

I oddly enough felt tired myself.

Katie must have been reading my mind because she said, "You seriously can't be tired after just waking up."

"Must be this wonderful food," I said as I winked at her. "Regardless, I think I'm going to head to bed as well. It will take me a while to fall asleep in a new place."

I headed back to my room and lay down on my bed. *What an interesting place*, I thought to myself before closing my eyes for the night.

6

Operation Black Flame

I WOKE UP to the sound of a bell ringing. I sprang up in bed and looked to my left. George, Kevin, and Sal were all slowly rolling out of bed and getting ready.

"What the heck is that?" I asked.

"That is your alarm clock," said Kevin with a chuckle.

"You guys use the fire alarm to wake up every morning?"

"No, jjjjjust Monday tttthrough Friday," Sal said, heading out the door.

Right, I highly doubt assassins have weekends off. I grabbed my shoes from the floor and put them on swiftly and made my bed in the same fashion as everyone had next to me. I left the room and started down the corridor when I heard Raven.

"Oh, good morning, Andy. How did you sleep?" She was standing there, smiling with her eyes still closed and her hair all over the place.

"I would assume not as well as you," I said, but I think I embarrassed her because she took off running to the bathroom.

"What are you doing just standing there? Come on," I heard George say as he grabbed my arm and dragged me down to the dining room.

We all sat down and enjoyed our breakfast. As we were finishing up, George looked at me and said, "It's your first mission today, boy." He grinned at me. "I have a wonderful little gift for you to take with you as well...Just in case."

"Andrew, come with me," Dragutin said, waiting in the doorway of the dining hall.

"Yes, sir," I said and jumped out of my seat to follow his lead.

"Now you get to have some fun," he said, smiling. "What do you know about the current tension between the United States and the Soviet Union?"

"Not a lot. They didn't really talk much about it in school," I said, kind of confused.

"Well, let's just say that they are both the world's strongest countries right now." He was talking while he was walking very briskly toward the end of the corridor. "We don't really partake in sides when it comes to war or conflicts. We simply follow the money...or potential flow of money." We approached the end of the corridor, and he put his hand on the wall.

"I always forget which one it is," he said, moving his hand over the concrete when suddenly his hand gave way.

I heard a grinding noise as the wall pulled backward and slid to the side.

"A secret room?" I asked.

"Of course. This is where we conduct mission planning," he said.

The room was vast and full of bookshelves along the walls. There was a giant table in the middle of the room in the shape of a pentagon, and they called it the Wanted Board. We approached the table and I saw the others were already coming into the room and forming around the table. I looked toward the center and saw a paper with the title bolded: OPERATION BLACK FLAME.

"What's Operation Black Flame?" I asked.

"Why your first mission, of course," Dragutin said happily.

I was not sure what the details were going to be, but it had a cool name, so I was already excited.

"You are going to assassinate a Soviet oligarch by the name of Olaf Yahontov. He is currently funneling a lot of money to the Soviet military, and the United States doesn't like that," Dragutin said. "What you need to know about this mission is that there is a specific way the US wants us to contract this hit."

"How is that?" I asked.

"He has to die in public," he said.

"You want me to assassinate a Soviet oligarch…in public? For my first mission?" I spouted.

This is a big deal, I thought. *Usually people take years to build up to a mission like this.*

"I expect great things from you, Andrew, so of course. You are your father's son, don't forget," he said, placing his hand on my shoulder.

I still thought it was crazy how he knew so much about my father and I apparently did not.

"Use your new team members to help complete the hit," Dragutin said as he left the room. "Oh, and good luck, boy."

I looked around the room, and everyone was staring at me like I should have known what I was supposed to do.

"Right, then, what have you got for me?" I looked at Raven first and she blushed. *Why does she do that?* I thought. *Anytime I am near her, her face gets red.*

"Well, I took care of scouting out a route for you, Andy," she said. "There are many rooftops where you could get a shot off as he is gaining access to his buildings. There are also many stops he makes throughout the day, from business meetings to lunches with other oligarchs. He has many bodyguards who protect him on his daily routine as well," she exclaimed.

A rooftop snipe might be good, but I would rather be up close and personal. Maybe if there was a crowded area he typically frequented.

"Which are the restaurants he attends?" I asked Raven.

"There are a couple different ones, but his favorite is a tavern he goes to in the evenings to eat with his old war comrades."

Perfect, I could pull a hit off in a food joint easily.

"Kevin, do you happen to have any poisons that I could use on this mission?" I asked him.

"Of course, there's a couple different opportunities you could have," he said. "If you are going to a tavern, you could place a poison in his drink or food. I have others that you can directly inject. I have ones that are powder, and if you get it in his airway he will swell like a watermelon." He giggled at the last one, kind of sinisterly.

"Uh, yeah, let's just go with an herb form I could put in a

food. But let me have an injectable version, too, just in case I'm made," I told him.

"I would suggest our water hemlock that we have in stock. It takes about sixty minutes to take effect, but when it does it will be too late. The person will experience nausea or abdominal pain and even seizures and vomiting, eventually leading to death," he said excitedly.

"Perfect. George, didn't you tell me you had something for me earlier as well?" I asked.

"Oh yes, I am very proud of this one, Mr. Andrew," he said with a crazy look in his eye. "This suitcase right here. All you have to do is put the pin 6-9-2-4-3 into the side, and this sucker will go off in about sixty seconds…give or take a few. I highly suggest you aren't anywhere close to it when it goes off."

"I'll keep that in mind, George, thank you." I could not think of anything else that I would need from anyone else. "All right, then, I supposed I'll be on my way" I said.

I grabbed the notes from Raven and the papers regarding other information on Mr. Yahontov and went back to my room. I opened my wall locker and readied my gear for the mission. I made sure my knife was sharp just in case I ran into any trouble. I also decided to have an AK-74 ready on standby in case that bomb was needed for some reason. I was hoping I wouldn't end up in a full-on war zone doing this job.

"I'll pack them and have them moved for you, sir," Katie said as she gathered my gun and suitcase.

We made our way down the corridor and rounded the corner to the elevator. We took the elevator up to what seemed over thirty floors.

"Wow, we were really underground, weren't we?" I said, astonished.

"Wouldn't be much of an assassin ring if people could just waltz right in, now would it?" Katie said.

"I suppose you are right," I said as the elevator stopped and we had made it to the garage.

"Right, Master Dragutin said that he has a friend who owes him one in the military, so you'll be taking one of their planes from the airport to the Soviet Union," Katie said.

"They are just going to let a US plane fly into their territory, no questions asked?" I said.

"Of course not, we aren't that dumb. It's a Soviet plane that they had hijacked," she said as she put my things into the vehicle. "Good luck, sir, and may shadows keep you hidden." She turned around and headed back to the elevator, and the doors shut behind her.

I got in the back seat of the car, and the driver headed off for the airport. The Western Sanctuary was located deep in the mountains of West Virginia, where the locals would not suspect us. It was so beautiful here; I never had seen such beautiful mountains and trees. I was remembering the island that I had lived on since the day I was born. On the way there, I was reading more on Mr. Yahontov and noticed that he had a wife and three children. He'd been a war hero during World War II, and apparently, he had been awarded the Order of Victory while being one of the main military officers during the siege of Berlin. He had much influence when it came to the military for this reason and for the constant flow of money that he's been adding to many of the oligarch's pockets to further his gains.

"Sir, we are here," the driver said.

I exited the vehicle and grabbed my things. The Soviet plane was already fired up and ready to go.

"You must be Dragutin's friend," the airman said as we approached the plane.

"Yes, I am," I said.

"Right, then, let's get this show on the road. I suggest you sleep on the way there. It will be a long flight with a couple stops," he said as we climbed into the plane.

I did as he said, though, and decided to take a nap on the flight to the Soviet Union. When I woke up, we were landing at Supino Air Base, which was a military transit base for the Soviet Union. I grabbed my briefcase and tucked my knife into my waistband.

"I'm actually going to leave that gun with you," I told the pilot.

"Not a problem, sir. I'll take real good care of it," he said, looking at it happily.

I made my way across the airstrip and toward the exit of the airfield. None of the soldiers noticed anything strange about me, luckily. I had a disguise to somewhat blend in with the common folk of the streets of Moscow. I made my way to a hotel that was directly across from the local tavern that Mr. Yahontov frequented. I chose the room on the third floor facing the street side so I could observe exactly what time he entered the establishment each night and about how long he would stay there. He seemed to be very punctual and arrive by car every evening by 1900 hours. He would be in the establishment for any time between sixty to seventy-five minutes.

The road seemed to be well populated with townsfolk passing through on their way to work. *That should work well for the hemlock to take effect*, I thought. *Now what to do with the armed guards.* There seemed to be six guards with him constantly and three vehicles. Two guards were in the first vehicle, two guards and Mr. Yahontov rode in the middle vehicle, and two followed in the rear. After a couple nights of plotting, I decided to make my way into the tavern to learn the layout of the building itself. I decided to go earlier in the day before Mr. Yahontov and friends would be there. I entered the building and noticed the tavern was not entirely big. There was a main bar that ran along the left side and then about ten tables on the left side with unsteady-looking chairs. However, in the far back, there was a marvelous-looking polished oak table and wooden chairs with cushions on them. *That must be where he sits*, I thought. I looked for the kitchen entrance and found it was about twenty feet or so from the table. I approached the barmaid and asked her for a menu:

"Могу я посмотреть меню, пожалуйста?" I was glad I knew several different languages; it definitely came in handy with this line of work.

"Конечно," she said with a smile.

I was observing the menu and noticed Yahontov's Pelmeni; it was a meat dumpling that was apparently Yahontov's favorite dish. I could easily place the hemlock petals crushed on top of the pelmeni to make it look like a garnish. *I think I have everything ready to go*, I thought. *Now I just must get the bomb in place.* I went back to my room at the hotel and waited for Olaf to show up with his armed guards. I had my suite case set for 6-9-2-4-2 in preparation to move the last roller to 3 when the time came. As soon as I saw them pull in, I grabbed my suitcase and made my way downstairs and out to the road. As I approached the other side of the road, I purposely tripped over the curb, dropping the suitcase under the middle car.

"Смотри, что ты делаешь, дурак," one of the guards standing outside said to me rather aggressively.

It worked—they thought I was just a clumsy fool. I told them sorry, "Извините," and made my way into the tavern.

Mr. Yahontov was seated at his table with three others of his military comrades. There were two guards standing by the table observing the tavern. I wondered where the other two guards ran off to. I was looking around the tavern and could not seem to find them. *Well, this could be a problem*, I thought to myself. Maybe this will not go as I planned. I ordered some food so that I would not seem suspicious being in the tavern and not eating. I made sure I ordered the pelmeni. When it arrived, I placed the hemlock petals all around the dish and on top of the pelmeni. I yelled in disgust after faking a bite of the dish, saying, "это мерзко," as I spit my pelmeni onto the ground.

Apparently, it got Olaf's attention because he was giving me a death glare.

"что не так, товарищ, иди сюда," he said, waving me to come over to his table with a look of confusion on his face.

I brought the plate over with me and told him how this dish was not as good as his looked.

"Ерунда, держу пари, на вкус она такая же, как у меня," he said as he stabbed a fork into one of the pelmeni on my plate and ate it.

The plan worked: he ate some of the hemlock. He chewed and began to make a scrunched face.

"Oof," he said after swallowing the bite and taking a swig of water.

He pointed to a chair and had one of the guards bring it over to their table. Apparently, I was invited to eat with them. He looked at the barmaid and ordered her to make another dish of his famous pelmeni for me to enjoy. I looked at my watch and was paying close attention so that I would not be here when the hemlock took its course. The pelmeni arrived, and it seemed even better than the last plate before I had put hemlock on it.

"Копаться в," I said, giving him a thumbs-up as I chewed up the dumpling. After a while of listening to their war stories and pretending to have been in the Soviet military myself, I looked down at my watch. It had been sixty minutes already. I looked back up, and Olaf's face was turning red, and he was beginning to sweat. I picked my glass up and spilled the liquid all over myself on purpose.

"Черт, я сейчас вернусь," I said as I got up from the table, wiping my pants off with the tablecloth.

I made my way to the door and heard Olaf begin to cough. *I may be in trouble here*, I thought; I walked a bit faster toward the door and left the building. *I must time this perfectly*, I thought to myself as I approached the car. I made sure my foot came down on the dial of the suitcase when I stepped down from the curb. I did it so my toe would hit the last combination and change the 2 to a 3 on the case. I continued to walk across the street like nothing had happened. I made it across the street and turned around; the door was slammed open, and Olaf was being helped to his car by two of the guards. He was a rather large man, so it was hard to get him into the back seat of the car. I started to walk toward the lobby of the hotel, and as I made it in, I heard the engines of the cars start. But only two vehicles started up. Where had those two guards gone? At this point I was knocked to the ground by a blast wave. The bomb had gone off and had clearly worked in its mission of publicly taking out Mr. Yahontov. I got up off the ground and quickly made my way upstairs to my room. The door was opened already, but I could have sworn I put the no room service sign up. I opened the door and saw one of the guards from Yahontov's convoy standing next to my desk with the papers about Olaf spread out across the surface. *Wait. Where's the second…* Too late. By the time I realized the second one was behind me, he had knocked me out.

7
Welcome to the Vorkuta Gulag

I OPENED MY eyes and was bound to a chair again, finding myself surrounded by concrete. My legs were bound to the legs of the chair and my wrists to the arms. There was a table directly in front of me and a double-sided mirror behind it. There were two chairs behind the table on the other side, and a heavy iron door on the right side of the room. Did I just find myself being captured by Olaf's men? *This will not end well for me*, I thought. *I need to plan an escape before they torture me for life*. I had heard horror stories of what happens to POWs and those who were captured completing different assassinations over different times. Of course, it varied from country to country, but the Soviet Union—they treated their prisoners the worst.

Slam.

The iron door swung open, and two men in Soviet military uniforms walked into the room. One was smoking a cigarette as he entered.

"Вы даже не представляете, насколько вы облажались прямо сейчас," the man said as he walked toward me.

"English, please," I said, looking up to him.

The one standing on the opposite side of the table began to laugh. The one closest to me looked at me in the eyes, puffing his cigarette.

"I'm Klasovich, and I'm in charge of the Vorkuta Gulag," he said. "Do you smoke?"

"No," I said, looking up at him.

"Shame," he said, putting out the cigarette on the side of my neck.

"Welcome to the Gulag." He snorted. "You will most likely enjoy your stay here. Seeing your line of work you do."

The soldier from across the table opened a folder he had with him, and it contained all the papers I had regarding Olaf and his assassination.

"We have no way of linking this to the Americans, but I can assure you, we know they are behind this," Klasovich said as he sat on the edge of the table. "You know, we could always use more operatives…if you would want to tell us anything helpful."

I glared at him, still feeling the burn on my neck. "Do your worst. I've been trained to take any types of torture you put before me," I said confidently to him. He looked down to my fingers and noticed that some of the fingernails were already missing from graduation day.

"You have it all wrong. I won't be torturing you at all. In fact, we let you all do that to each other. How many people have you killed in your life? You seem…young," he said, looking at me as if I was a child.

"Enough to know that you are next if you don't let me out of these binds," I snapped back at him.

"Ha, he's got spirit, doesn't he, Ivan?" Klasovich said as they both laughed.

"You are going to make me a lot of money," he said as he patted me on the back. "Ivan, go grab his knife, would you?" The soldier stepped out of the room and came back with my knife. "You are probably pretty handy with this," Klasovich said as Ivan handed him the knife, and he began twirling it in his hand.

Klasovich was an older man, was clean shaven, and had neatly cut gray hair. Ivan seemed much younger, and he had brown hair and was kind of fat for a soldier. Klasovich approached me with the knife, keeping eye contact with me each step he took, disconcertingly slow.

"How about we see what you are made of," he said as he cut the bindings from my legs and wrists.

I could easily kill him right now if I am quick enough, I thought. *Ivan would be an easy target straight after. However, I have no idea what floor I am on. Let alone how big this building even is and how many other soldiers are inside this prison.* He helped me stand up and gave me a shove toward the door.

"Move!" he snarled as we walked out of the room.

I closed my left eye as if I had something in it and forced it to stay closed. As we entered the hall, my heart sank: there were many soldiers. *Looks like I will not be escaping this place anytime soon.* We passed by a couple different rooms, and then I heard screaming. I was taken to the end of the hallway, where there was a stairwell, and we began walking down the stairs.

We went down about two floors, and then we entered another hallway and proceeded into a small room off to the side of it. Ivan handed me the knife, and I clenched my fingers around it. His hands were very cold, and he pulled me close to him.

"You will never leave this place. But the more you win, the longer you get to stay alive." Then he let go of me and left the room. I heard them close a cage door behind me and lock it.

"Good luck," Ivan said rather sarcastically. The room I was in was rather dark and smelled horrid. *What am I supposed to do now?* I thought to myself. I opened my left eye, which was adjusted to the dark since it had been closed on the way to the room. I made out the outline of the room, and there seemed to be a door in front of me. I looked to the left corner, and there was a pile of something. I approached it and the smell got worse—bodies. *Seems these guys were not so lucky.* I turned back to the door that I originally found and saw there was a slight breach of light coming from under the door. I raised my unarmed hand to the door and gave it a slight push so it gave way in front of me. I heard loud screams of cheering and booing, an equal mixture of the two, as I entered the room. I looked around and saw I was in some sort of pit; above me were balconies all the way around the room, and there were many soldiers. They were the ones cheering and booing, it would seem. I looked down at my knife and rubbed my thumb across the handle and the initials V.G.B.

"Shadows protect my back and luck guide my blade, Father," I said quietly to myself.

This was his blade from when he was younger and a field operative. Dragutin had had it in my locker waiting for me when I arrived at the Sanctuary. I looked back up and saw that there was another door on the other side of the room being opened. A man was walking out in ragged clothing that had been torn in multiple spots. He had no hair, and filth covered his body; the crowd went nuts when this guy came in the room. I think this was the first time I missed being back on the island, where it was warm and my father and dog were waiting for me after school.

"Ahhh! I will drink your blood!" the man screamed, and the soldiers absolutely lost their minds at this.

They were cheering, "Жнец! Жнец! Жнец!" Reaper? This guy apparently had a nickname. Seemed like a kind of lame one, though. I started to walk toward this Reaper character, and he did the same. However, he seemed to be increasing his pace the closer he got, and I then realized that he was planning on a rush. I dodged to the left as he missed and caught himself before falling to the ground. He spun back around, and I finally got a good look at his face. He had about three teeth missing, and almost all of them leftover were chipped. He had a giant gash going down the right side of his face, and his ear was completely missing. He began to make beast-like noises and growl toward me. *Is this guy even human anymore?* I thought. *He seems more like a savage animal.* He lunged quickly and knocked me to the ground. My knife fell out of my hands just a short reach from grabbing distance. *This isn't good*, I thought as he began punching me in the face. I deflected the majority of the punches and then threw a counterpunch landing on his kidneys. He grunted as he fell off of me, and I crawled toward my knife. I stood back up as quickly as possible to avoid my back being taken. He was holding his side as he stood up, and he was staring at me and drooling at this point.

"Ahh!" he bellowed as he charged at me with brute force. He again managed to knock the knife from my hands, but this time it didn't fall too far from me. It landed between both of our feet. He was quick but not quick enough: I countered him by grabbing his arm and sweeping his legs from under him. *Crash*. He landed face-first on some debris that had fallen from the ceiling many years before.

"Pity," I said as I brought my foot down on the back of his head. The way his face was positioned on the rock, his mouth was open and gripping it. When the foot came down, it knocked the remaining teeth from his skull. He let a squeal out, and I saw his body begin to shake. At first, I thought it was out of fear, but then I quickly realized it was because he was laughing. I picked up the knife and crouched down over him. He rolled over, and I grabbed his collar, bringing the knife close to his neck. At this point he was staring at me and smiling. I slowly sank the knife into his neck and then quickly tore it through. He convulsed for a couple of seconds and then went limp. *I do not want to become like him*, I thought. *I need to find a way out of this horrid place.* I looked around the balcony, and the soldiers were going insane. At this point I heard a door open from where I had originally entered, and two Soviet soldiers approached me.

"Пойдем," grunted one of them rather angerly.

So I walked toward them, but they reached for their pistols.

"Нож," they both screamed at me.

I realized I was still holding my knife and they were

concerned I would stab them next. I dropped it to the ground and raised my arms above my head. They approached me and gave me a shove toward the door. We passed back through the dark room and proceeded back into the hallway. Instead of making a left back toward the stairs, we made a right this time. We rounded a corner, and I could see multiple stories of cells. Many people were talking to each other and in different languages. Eventually we came to a stop, and I was shoved into an open cell. They slid the cell door shut and locked it, then proceeded to walk away. I seemed to be on the ground floor from what I could tell. I turned around and noticed I had a cellmate, apparently. Sitting on the bunk staring at me, he was a skinny man and had long brown hair and a raggedy beard with very sad brown eyes. He seemed to have been here for a while, by the looks of it.

"English?" he said.

"Yes. Hello, what's your name?"

"Douglas, but my friends call me Doug," he said.

"I'm Andrew, pleasure to meet you," I said as I looked at the rest of the cell's layout. It was rather small—Doug was sitting on the ground in the corner. He seemed to be content. There was a bucket a little farther from him in the opposite corner. There was no furniture in this cell, just a bucket, which I assumed stunk.

"You must have killed Reaver," he said quietly. "He was my old cellmate. He was a very crazy man."

"I made sure it was painless," I said as I looked into his eyes. "Why are you here?" I asked him.

"I was an American soldier once, that was nine years ago.

While we made our way inland toward Germany, I met a beautiful young woman. She was a Soviet, but I had no idea she was anyone important. One thing led to another, and she became pregnant. I wanted her to come with me and for us to get married, and she happily agreed. Unfortunately, her father was a rather high-ranking officer in the Soviet military. I went to her house one day to bring her with me, because we were moving out of Germany. He showed up with many soldiers, and they brought me here. Apparently, she was supposed to have an arranged marriage to another." He seemed very sad about the situation.

"Well, if you stick with me, we will be out of here shortly," I said to him confidently. His face lit up like he'd been given a Christmas present.

"That would mean everything to me," he said as a tear rolled down the side of his face.

8

Escape from Vorkuta

I WAS STANDING by the edge of the cell, looking out from it, trying to calculate my best approach for getting out of this cesspit.

"So what did you do?" Doug said to me.

"What?" I said to him, confused because I was clearly focused on devising a plan.

"What did you do to get brought in here?" he asked curiously.

"I assassinated a Soviet oligarch by the name of Olaf Yahontov," I said bluntly.

His eyes widened as I said this. "You...you...killed him?" He acted like I had just told him the world was going to end. "Do you have any...Why would you do such a crazy thing?" he said.

"I was ordered to," I told him.

"Wait, what do you mean you were ordered to? Were you a soldier too?" he asked.

I turned to him with a rather serious face and said, "Yeah, let's go with that."

Doug seemed nice enough, but there was something fishy about him. I also did not feel like divulging years of secrets on how our organization was set up and famous hits we had carried out.

"How often do guards pass through here?" I asked.

"Hmm. I'd say probably about once a day," he said.

"I'm assuming it's to bring us food?" I said.

"Yeah, you get one meal a day. It's usually moldy bread. Sometimes it's soggy for some reason." He made a scrunched face.

"You get used to the taste of it, though. Oh yeah, when you are done with the bucket, make sure you dump it out the cell to the right. There is a drain that leads down," he said, scratching his neck.

"Any idea where it leads?" I asked curiously.

"No idea, but I wouldn't want to crawl into it if I were you. You'd probably just die from standing in the fumes," he exclaimed.

That was a valid point; I'd rather not try to escape and end up getting some illness from the toxic air and waste that flowed through the channels.

"How many times have you fought?" I asked him.

"Only about once a week," he said.

Once a week, for nine years—that is a lot of fighting, I thought. *This guy must be stronger than he looks.* I felt so trapped, and my head was swirling with ideas on how I could possibly get out of this place. I looked at the bucket in the corner and noticed there was a small wire for the handle. *That will do perfectly*. I made my way to it and began to try and remove it from the bucket.

"Hey now, we are lucky to have that on there. It helps dumping," he said angrily.

"Do you want to get out of here? Or have the nicest bucket in the gulag?" I said to him coldly.

He slouched back down into the corner and rolled his eyes.

"Look, I appreciate the false motivation you gave me about getting out of this place. It won't work, though. Look around you. We are absolutely trapped in this hellhole. I don't think I've ever heard of anyone making it out of this place," he said, rather defeated.

"Well, apparently your brain doesn't work like mine," I said as I gave him a wink.

Then he sighed and stared at me as I continued to try and break the wire free from the bucket.

Snap.

"All right, lookee there. We are in business." I chuckled. "Just one more side."

I was twisting and pulling on the other side until it finally came free as well.

"So what are you going to do with that? Make a wire shank?" he said, moving his hands in front of him, mocking me.

"So what if I am?" I told him.

"They will find it," he said.

"I doubt it. How often do they actually talk to us?" I asked.

"I mean, they order us around when we go to fight. But other than that, they don't," he said.

"Exactly," I said. "It's easy to pretend you have no idea what they are saying either. I can easily just not say anything."

"What are you getting at?" he said to me curiously.

"Just have faith in me, and I'll get us out of here, okay?" I stuck my hand out to him to give him a promising handshake. He stared at it for a second and then looked up at me.

"Deal," he said, as he shook my hand.

I heard yelling from all the cells and got up to look out the side of the bars. "They are coming already?" I asked Doug.

"Yeah, chow time," he said as he stood up and came toward the cell door as well.

I folded the wire four times and tucked it in the back of my waistband, where it was not easily visible. The soldiers finally made it to our cell, and they had a basket full of moldy bread. I noticed that one of them had a key ring along the right side of his waist.

"Cheeseburger," one of them said, chuckling as they tossed one piece of the moldy bread past us, into the corner.

Doug leapt at it immediately and scarfed it down. The guards continued past the cell and down the line, handing out bread to other captives.

"Really?" I said to him, holding out my arms.

"Sorry, Reaver and I used to fight over the food," he said while he blushed.

I went back to the corner I had recently claimed and sat down. I pulled the wire from the back of my pants and began shaping it. Doug looked at me, rather intrigued, as I formed a small shank with the wire. I folded it in such a way that the wire had two ends twisted together jutting out from between my middle finger and index finger. I then began to scratch the concrete with it, trying to sharpen the ends of the wire.

"Someone was a Boy Scout," said Doug with a chuckle.

"I don't even know what that is," I said to him, rather confused.

"What did you grow up on—an island?" he said, laughing.

"Yes," I said to him as I continued to file down the wire.

"What? So you aren't from the United States?" he asked, perplexed.

"I'm from an island out in the Pacific Ocean. No one really knows about it; I promise I'll explain everything when we get out of here," I told him.

He looked at me like I was some sort of alien or I was telling a lie. Either way he just sighed and said, "All right, well, enjoy arts and crafts. I am going to sleep for the night. I like to sleep on a full stomach." He rolled over onto his side, facing away from me.

I finished my shank and tucked it back into my pants and lay down to go to sleep as well. I woke up the next morning to what sounded like rain. I opened my eyes, almost forgetting where I was.

"Morning," Doug said as he was peeing in the bucket that was next to my head.

"Are you serious?" I said as I jumped off the ground.

"I didn't want to move the bucket and wake you," he said, laughing.

I looked out the cell door again and was looking down the hallway on either side of the cellblock. Did not seem like any guards were on patrol right now. Then I saw someone familiar rounding the corner. Ivan and one other guard were heading right to our cell. I backed up slightly, and Ivan approached the door.

"Hey there, comrade," he said with an evil grin on his face. "Ready for your next fight?" he said excitedly.

I looked at Doug and sighed. "I thought you said one fight a week?" I snapped at him.

"That's for everyone else," Ivan said, as he lit up a cigarette in front of me. He puffed it and then blew some smoke in my face.

"You are a special breed, and you were born to fight. You get to go every day, lucky you," he said as he took another puff from his death stick.

"Open her up!" Ivan shouted as the henchman fumbled to grab his keys and unlock the cell door.

"Oh yeah, bring the friend," Ivan said, pointing at Doug.

"But I already fought this week," Doug said, rather cowardly.

"Shut it," Ivan scolded Doug.

We both left the cell and followed Ivan with the other guard at our rear. I was directly behind Ivan, and we were heading for the small room I had been in the other day before my last fight. As we approached the room, Ivan turned toward me and said,

"In you go." The door had already been opened, waiting for our arrival.

I fell, pretending to have tripped over a loose stone on the ground.

"Get up," Ivan snarled as he kicked my rib. Unlucky for him, that is what I was planning on. I caught his foot under my arm and quickly twisted toward him, pulling him off-balance. The man let out a yelp as he toppled toward the ground. Doug saw his chance as well and elbowed the other guard in the stomach, knocking the wind from him. I shot up Ivan's leg and retrieved the shank I had made earlier. I brought it close to his carotid artery and was inches from his face. Doug had gotten the other guard in a choke hold and snapped his neck. He let the limp body fall to the floor.

"Now, you listen to me," I snarled at Ivan. "You are going to tell me the fastest way out of this place. After that I'll let you go."

Ivan must not have been one for threats, because he was breathing rather heavily and sweating. "Ri-right...take my ID card in my left breast pocket," he said, and I retrieved it from the pocket. "Then...then...you want to make it to the top floor. We have a helicopter on standby constantly in case Klasovich needs to leave in a hurry," he stammered.

That's all I needed to hear. I sank the shank into his neck and sliced up to his jawline to make sure the artery would open vertically.

"Now's our chance Doug," I told him as I began taking my clothes off.

"Oh, good idea," Doug said as he began to do the same.

We put both of the soldier's uniforms on and dragged the two onto the pile of bodies that had been in the dark room. We made our way to the stairs and began our ascent.

"We have to be quick, Doug," I told him as I looked back to see him closely following me. We made it to the top of the building, and there was a sign on a door in front of us labeled "Крыша."

Perfect, we made it to the roof. I slammed open the door, and the helicopter was indeed on the helipad. "Get in!" I yelled to Doug as we ran to the helicopter. I hopped in the pilot's seat, and the dashboard looked rather foreign to me.

"Do you know how to fly?" Doug said in a panic.

"Uh…no…" I said.

"Switch me spots!" he bellowed.

At that point we heard a siren begin to sound throughout the whole prison. *We are out of time*, I thought. *We need to get moving immediately.*

"Hurry!" I yelled at Doug as he fired up the bird.

He started flipping many different switches, and the roof began to give a rather vicious purr. We began to lift off when the door slammed back open on the building's roof. Klasovich and eight other guards were running out of the stairwell onto the roof.

"Shoot it down!" Klasovich yelled, pointing at the helicopter, and I saw all eight of the guards point their AK-74s directly at us.

"Hold on!" yelled Doug as he yanked the yoke of the helicopter, and we flew rather quickly up and back.

Ting. Ting. Ting.

I heard as a couple bullets hit the side of the helicopter. The bullets eventually stopped hitting us as we quickly made it out of range.

"We…we actually did it," Doug said, surprised.

"Yes, now we need to get out of this country!" I yelled to him.

"I know just the spot! We are going to Poltava Air Base!" he yelled over the roaring sound of the helicopter.

9

A New Recruit

"WE ARE almost there!" Doug yelled over the very loud propellers.

I saw the air base in perfect view and was starting to wonder if the Sanctuary thought I had died. Doug brought the bird in and down onto a landing zone gently and powered it down. There were many US troops approaching the helicopter at this point.

"You boys lost?" an older man said as he approached us with armed guards.

This guy looked like he was probably important. I noticed the men around him were very nervous and that the guy had two stars on his uniform. A general—hopefully Doug knows this guy. The general had blond hair and blue eyes. You could tell he worked out even though he was the age where he probably should not. He had a very thin mustache, which was kind of amusing.

"By God! Dougie, is that you?" The general said. Dougie? I began to laugh at that, and Doug gave me a punch on the shoulder.

"Long time no see, Collyn," he said as they gave each other a hug.

"This is one of my friends, Andrew," Doug said, pointing at me. "He helped me escape Vorkuta."

Collyn's eyes widened. "How did you manage to do that?" He took a step to the side and leaned his head to see the helicopter behind us. "Looks like someone had some target practice on you two," he said with a grin. "Well, let's get you guys to the barracks. You could use a shower…a long one," he said with a scrunched face.

We made our way to the barracks located within the air base. They seemed to be very nice and well maintained. I showered and changed into some extra clothes Collyn had brought us.

"Ready to go?" Doug said as he was combing his hair.

"Yes, I really need to get back to the Sanctuary," I said.

"Right, you have to tell me about all of that here soon," he said as we left the barracks and headed for the general's lodge.

The brick building had marvelous pillars supporting the roof hanging over the entryway of the small mansion. I knocked on the door, and Collyn answered it in more comfortable-looking clothes.

"Come in!" he said as we walked through the front door.

The floors were all wooden and polished. There seemed to be many rooms in this place and a staircase that spiraled from the entryway.

"This way," he said as we followed him into what looked like a library. "Have a seat, gentlemen," he said, pouring scotch into three glasses. "I thought you were dead for the longest time, Doug," Collyn said, taking a sip of the scotch.

"Yeah, I basically felt like it," Doug said, also sipping some of the scotch.

"It's been nine years. You were in Vorkuta for that long and survived. That itself is an accomplishment," Collyn said.

"I'm aware. Last time I saw you, you were just a captain," Doug said, smiling.

There was an awkward silence for a moment, and then Collyn said, "Look, Doug, I'm not sure what you had to go through in Vorkuta, and I'd rather not have you dwell on it. But quickly move on from it—how would you like to be my second?"

"You want me to be the one-star on post?" Doug said.

"Yes," Collyn said.

"I kind of have other commitments that I need to see through first, unfortunately," Doug said, looking then toward me.

"Right, I can only imagine the debt you have to pay to this young man," he said, nodding toward me.

"As far as the military is concerned, you died nine years ago and have a headstone and everything. So you are basically a ghost," Collyn said.

This is perfect, I thought. *If he is assumed dead, he could join us at the Sanctuary. It would be a little unorthodox having an outsider in the organization, but it is still possible. I need people I trust and know after my capture took place.*

"I appreciate it, Collyn," Doug said, taking another sip of his scotch. "I'd also like one more favor."

"What would that be?" asked Collyn.

"You think you could hook us up with transport back to the States?" Doug said.

"Certainly, where are you two heading?" he asked, looking at the two of us.

"West Virginia," I said to him.

"Not much to do out there except hunting," Collyn said, drinking down the last of his scotch. "I'll have the plane set up for you gentlemen immediately," he said as he stood up. "Let me make a phone call, and I'll make sure we have a plane fueled up and ready to go." Collyn left the room, and Doug looked at me.

"You can tell me all about where we are going and what your story is on the way there," he said as he downed the last of his scotch.

"Oh yes, I'm going to tell you everything," I said.

"Right, I'll take you two to the airplane. We had one getting ready to head that direction already," Collyn said, entering the room.

I downed the rest of my scotch, and we made our way from the lodge back to the airstrip. A plane was fired up and ready to go.

"Hey! I know you!" the pilot yelled at me as we approached the plane.

"Ah yes, do you still have my gun by chance?" I asked him.

"Oh yeah, it shoots like a champ," he said, giving me a thumbs-up. We waved to Collyn as we got onto the plane.

"I'll be back soon! I promise," said Doug as we closed the plane door.

We took our seats across from one another, and the plane began to take off.

"Well," Doug said, staring at me impatiently.

"Where should I begin?" I said and then paused for a moment. "It all started when I was ten years old. Up until then I had lived on an island with my father and dog, living a completely normal life. I went to a typical school and learned typical things, but it all changed that day I turned ten."

"What do you mean?" Doug asked.

"Well, you see, this wasn't just a typical island. I and many other children were specifically brought there at a very young age to be conditioned and accepted into Black Fawn Academy," I said.

"I've never heard of it," Doug said, scratching his head.

"Most people haven't. It is a school that trains you in the ways of being an assassin so that you can be used by any government needing a helping hand with toppling a regime, rebuilding order, boosting economies, and so on. We even help the rich or whoever can pay for our services, really," I told him.

"So you grew up on an island and trained to be an assassin since you were ten," Doug said, wide-eyed.

"Yeah, I didn't have much of a life. I didn't get to experience culture like you have in the United States and other countries. I never played any sports or had sleepovers at friends' houses. But I could tell you anything you wanted to know about poisons. I can tell you anything you want to know about how much TNT I would need to take down a building. I can tell—"

"Okay, okay, I get it, hotshot," Doug said, laughing.

"Yeah, this was actually my first mission I went on," I said as I put my head down.

"Well, you seemed to have gotten the job done. Minus getting captured and all. But I'm glad you did! Or else I would have been stuck in that pit," he said happily. He sat there quietly for a few seconds and then began to speak. "Well, you heard my friend. The military and everyone I know thinks I'm dead…You guys need an extra hand?"

I thought back to the incident when I'd been initially captured and how the guards had known I was there for the hit. They had not stopped me until after I had completed it. I was supposed to be caught, I realized. Someone had reported it in to them.

"Yes, I will certainly need your help," I said to him.

Either I'd been betrayed by someone within the Sanctuary or this assignment was a complete setup by the buyer. We continued to talk on the flight home, and Doug made me aware of all the cool things I had missed out on during my childhood. After what felt like an eternity, we finally made it back to the States and to the airport. To my surprise the driver that had taken me to the airport initially was there waiting for us. We climbed out of the plane and made our way to the driver.

"Hey, Andrew, I heard you were on your way back from mission. Glad to see you are in one piece," said the driver, smiling. This was odd, and I wondered how the Sanctuary knew that I had made it out of the Soviet Union. Maybe they didn't know I had been captured at all.

"Thanks," I said to him as Doug and I got in the back seat. We took the long journey back through the woods and mountains of West Virginia. After another very long trip, we had finally made it home.

"Welcome to the Western Sanctuary," I said to Doug as we got out of the car in the garage. I approached the elevator and pressed the button.

"Seems a bit weird having an assassin group up in an old garage," Doug said, looking around, confused.

"Ring, it's an assassin ring," I said to him.

Ding.

The elevator door opened, we entered, and I pressed the button that said "S" on it. We began to descend rather quickly.

"How many floors are we passing right now?" Doug said, amazed.

"Many," I said, chuckling.

The elevator came to a halt, and the doors opened. We both stepped off and into the corridor.

"Very dark and gloomy place," Doug said, looking around as we made our way toward the secret room.

"Hhhello," a familiar chilling voice said from behind us.

"Ahh!" Doug screamed as he quickly turned around.

Sal had been creeping behind us since we had gotten off the elevator, apparently. He was standing there awkwardly, staring at Doug. No one said anything for a moment, and then Sal said, "Ccccan I take his ffffingernails?" as he licked his lips.

"No Sal, he's with us, you psycho," I said to him as I grabbed Doug's shoulder and moved him toward the secret room. Sal crept back into the shadows as we made our way to the room. I placed my hand on the wall in the spot I'd seen Dragutin touch previously to gain entry. The wall pushed back and slid open like before, and I saw Katie, Kevin, George, and Raven all standing around the Wanted Board.

"I heard my explosive worked pretty well," George said, rubbing his hands together and smiling.

"I heard you were captured," said Katie.

"He was, but my flock told me he escaped," Raven said, smiling.

"Who's that guy?" Kevin said.

They all were rushing me with questions all at once. "Everyone, stop," I said, and they all stopped talking and looked at me. "I'll explain everything just one at a time."

I told them about the entire mission and the complications with which I was captured and how we managed to escape.

"So he's a new recruit, then, it would seem," Raven said shyly.

"Exactly, seeing as I'm next in line to be master of the Sanctuary, I should be able to bring him in, right?" I said, and no one seemed to argue against my point.

"Where is Dragutin, anyway?" I asked, looking around the room.

"Yeah...about that," Katie said. "He uh...well...He went on a mission shortly after you did and was captured as well."

This is definitely not a coincidence, Dragutin and I both being captured in the act of completing our missions, I thought. *I think we have ourselves a mole; no wonder there was an inquisition recently.* I looked around the room at all the faces and was trying to figure out if it was possibly someone in this room.

"Well, let's not waste any time," I said as I leaned onto the Wanted Table. "We are going on a rescue mission."

10

Operation Dragon Thunder

"YOU WANT TO what?" Katie said, looking at me, confused. "You realize we aren't a rescue ring. We are an assassin ring." The others nodded in agreement with her.

"So what? You just want to leave Dragutin to die? Or be tortured and give away secrets?" I asked angrily.

"Well…no one came or attempted to rescue you," Kevin said quietly.

That was true: they'd left me for dead and had no intentions of ever seeing me again, apparently.

"We would have missed you, though," Raven said, blushing, and immediately looked at the ground.

"I know I'm new here," Doug stammered, "but I think Andy knows what's best for the Sanctuary, right? I mean from what he's told me he has had the most schooling and knowledge about how the assassin's world works compared to the rest of you."

"I suppose you are right," said Katie as she scratched the back of her head. "All I'm saying is that you should consider letting him go. After all, we have no idea where he is or what his mission was. He didn't tell us any of the details. He said it was private. However, when he didn't return in a day or two, we thought he may have been compromised. So we searched his desk and found this."

She handed me a piece of paper that was folded up. I opened it, and it was a short letter. I read it aloud so everyone could hear:

"Dragon, I need your help immediately. Tell no one where you are going, just that you were assigned a classified mission. There has been an attempt on my life, and the order is in danger. You must hurry, I am located at the spot of origination. —V.G.B." My heart sank; I knew those initials…*It can't be*, I thought. *I watched him die.*

"What's wrong?" Doug said, as he could see I was visibly shaken.

"I know who he went to see, but what I don't know is where this spot of origination is," I said, confused.

"Well, I don't know much about this place or your customs," Doug started. "Perhaps it's meaning the literal sense of the foundation of your order?"

Everyone shot glances at him.

"What…did I say something to offend you guys?" he said, looking around the room.

"No, that's a good idea, Doug," I said to him, "but I honestly have no idea where the order was initially founded."

I should have paid more attention in the history of the assassin world class.

"I...I think I might know where this place is," Raven said. "I remember we talked about a place of origin while at Falcon's Reach Academy. It's on an island somewhere in the Pacific Ocean." It couldn't possibly be.

"This is ridiculous. Hand me that map, Katie," I said, pointing across the Wanted Table at a map lying by her. She handed it to me, and I asked Raven to come stand next to me. Her face turned a deep red, and she did not move for a second. "What are you gawking at, weirdo? Get over here," I said to her. She rushed over to me and stood awkwardly far from me and was staring right at me. This girl was so strange.

"Is this where you were taught about this island?" I said as I put my finger down out in the Pacific Ocean.

"Yes, that looks very familiar to me," she said happily. I sighed.

"What's wrong?" said Katie. "Do you know where this place is after all?"

"Know it...I lived there my whole life," I said.

Everyone stopped talking for a moment, and awkward glances were passed around. "You mean, that's where that Black Fawn Academy is?" Doug asked.

"Yes," I said. "I also thought we had a mole within our Sanctuary when I found out that Dragutin and I were both captured on mission. However, I now realize that none of you is to blame for what happened."

"You aren't making any sense right now, Andrew," Kevin said to me, scrunching his face.

"The man who wrote this letter, I believe to be my father," I said. "Those initials at the end of this letter are his. His name is Vincenzo Giuseppe Bertolini."

"Well, at least we know where we are going now," George said.

"Yes, but that means someone has tried to kill Andrew's dad as well," Katie said.

"I think I know who is behind the destruction of the order," I said. "His name is Alexander Aminoff. He was a professor at Black Fawn Academy and a member of the Council."

"The Council?" Katie said, astonished.

"What's the Council?" Doug asked, confused more than ever.

"The Council are the earliest members who established our assassin order," said Kevin, "It is made up of nine individuals whose names are unknown to us lower members. They keep it that way in case any of the sanctuaries are overtaken or you get captured on mission."

"So that means two of the nine members are Master Dragutin and Andrew's Father," Doug stated.

"Yes," I said. "It also means that Aminoff is in the Council as well, which means we know three of them."

The room was quiet for a moment, and then I finally spoke.

"All right, looks like we are going on a little trip back to my home. We aren't going to be seen, though it needs to be a complete stealth mission if we are going to get this done right. We are going to rescue both Dragutin and my father from Aminoff."

"How exactly do you know this Aminoff guy is the one plotting against the Council?" asked Katie.

"I just know," I said, looking her in the eyes until she uncomfortably looked away.

"So what's the plan, then, Andrew?" said Kevin, looking at the map.

"Well, the best way to get to the island is by plane. But we will need to enter the island undetected," I said.

"We will have to parachute in, then?" said Katie.

"Exactly," I said.

"I can pilot the plane," Doug said happily.

"Great, the rest of us will be going as well," I said.

"All of us?" Katie said.

"Yes, I believe we will need each and every one of your talents in this room...even creepy watcher over there," I said, looking over to the darkest corner of the room, where Sal was hiding from the rest of us.

"Ffffinally, it's my time to sssshine," Sal said, giggling and remaining hidden from sight.

"Yeah, yeah, whatever. Anyways, the plan is we will parachute onto the island farthest from the academy. It is a very secure facility with guard towers, barbed-wire fences, and many different biometric devices that we must get past in order to gain entry to the facility. After we make entry, we should make our way on foot to my old house. I'm sure we will be able to find something regarding the Council in there," I said.

"Sounds like not a lot to go on and a lot to go wrong," Katie said with frown.

"It will work, I know it will," I said, looking around at all of them. I glanced to the corner, at the clock. "We need to head out in an hour if we are going to make landfall by night," I said as I began to leave the room.

Everyone went to their respective quarters and began gathering the items they needed to conduct their mission.

"Got a minute?" Doug said as we were leaving the room.

"Sure, what's on your mind?" I asked.

"So, um. What exactly will I be doing while you guys are on mission? I mean after I fly by and you all parachute out," he said.

That was a valid question, and I took a moment before responding to him.

"I think you should read those books in the secret room. They have tons of information on each respective line of work within the order," I told him. "I think you'll be able to comprehend all of it, and I'm really not sure how long we will all be gone. Who knows where we will end up after this."

"I think I can do that," he said, making an odd face. "I really hate reading, though." At that I laughed.

"Me too, Doug, me too," I said as I walked away and headed to my wall locker.

I grabbed another knife from the rack, seeing as my locker was full of various weapons. I also changed back into the order uniform and made sure my area was neat and tidy. After a while I made my way to the common area, where everyone was waiting for me.

"Let's get this show on the road," I said as everyone began to get up and follow me to the elevator.

We went up to the garage and took multiple cars to the airport. It was another long drive all the way back to the airport.

When we arrived, the pilot was coming out of his living quarters on base.

"Hey, guys, I didn't know you were going to need me again so soon. Give me a moment to get the plane all ready," he said.

"No worries, Doug here will be flying us this time," I said, smiling to him.

He looked at Doug and shrugged. "Just don't adjust the seat. I hate trying to get it back to perfect position," he said as he turned back around and headed to the pilots' quarters.

We all boarded the plane, and Doug got it ready for flight. We sat around in the back of the plane talking about other missions that the group had gone on before I showed up to the Sanctuary. The plane took off, and we were on our way to our destination. After a while of conversing and waiting, Doug yelled back to us, "Five minutes until drop!"

I made sure everyone's parachute was on right and ready to go.

"Sal...why have you not changed yet?" I asked him, rather annoyed. He was still wearing his monk-looking robe and red rope.

"Wwwwhy change when I ccccan be ccccomfortable?" he said quietly.

I rolled my eyes and made sure his rig was good to go like the rest of us.

"Thirty Seconds!" Doug yelled to us as the back door opened from the plane. I looked behind me to give everyone a thumbs-up, and they all returned one as well. The light on the back of the plane turned green, and we leapt one by one into the night sky of the tropical island. We made our descent toward the corner of the island that I'd spoken of to everyone earlier. It felt so freeing falling from the sky; it was an amazing rush but also godlike. We inched closer and closer toward the ground, and we pulled our chutes. We began to lower slowly and eventually made contact with the ground. We took the parachutes off and repacked them and put them in the bushes near the coast.

"Right, my house is this way," I said, as we began walking silently through the woods. We walked for about two hours before we made it to where I lived. We were standing in the wood line viewing my house. I had many memories pass though my head as I looked at it. I looked out to the yard and noticed nothing abnormal about the exterior. We advanced to the house, which had no lights on and was very quiet. *Slider must not be here*, I thought, *or he'd be going nuts by now*. Raven passed us and made her way to the sliding glass door as we lined up on the wall of the house. She picked the lock rather quickly, and we gained entry.

"Make yourselves comfortable," I said as I made my way to my father's bedroom. I entered the room and turned the lamp on by the bed. I made my way over to the desk and opened the top drawer. I saw a document pertaining to certain activities at the academy. *Mostly just work stuff, it seems*, I thought as I shuffled through the drawer. I closed the drawer and was beginning to walk away when I noticed something strange about the desk.

"Of course," I said, as I walked back toward the desk. I began feeling under the brim of the top and eventually felt a button. I pressed the button, and a secret panel popped off the side of the desk, and I saw a paper on the very top. I picked up the paper and saw there was a weird circular symbol located on it. It seemed very foreign to me, and I had no idea what it could possibly mean. *This has to be some sort of help to find where they are right now*, I thought. I brought the paper downstairs and found everyone was hanging out in my old living room.

"I found something," I said as I handed the paper to Katie.

"What is this symbol?" she said, just as confused as I was.

"I have no idea, but I guarantee that gives us our next lead," I said.

Raven began to walk toward the paper, and her eyes lit up. "That's the symbol of the Council!" she said excitedly. "What else is on it?" She looked around the paper, which seemed to be completely blank. "That's it! Andrew, go grab me some lemon juice from the kitchen and we also need a hair dryer," she said.

Of course, I thought to myself. There was a message with invisible ink somewhere on the paper. I grabbed the lemon juice from the kitchen and then went upstairs to my father's room. I entered his bathroom, hoping that one of his lovely ladies who have come and visited happened to have a hair dryer tucked away. I set the lemon juice on the bathroom sink and began rummaging through the cabinet below. I luckily found one among some other peculiar objects I wish I hadn't seen. I grabbed both the hair dryer and the lemon juice and rushed back downstairs. Raven and the others were gathered around the kitchen table.

"Oh, shoot, we need a cotton swab too," Raven said.

"I was just upstairs!" I said, annoyed, and made my way all the way back up the steps.

Back to the bathroom just to get the long-forgotten cotton

swab. I made my way back downstairs, and Raven had the hair dryer plugged in, the lemon juice in a bowl, and the kitchen light on. *So much for tactical recovery*, I thought to myself. She dabbed the cotton swab in the lemon juice and began rubbing the paper while applying heat with the air dryer. Nothing happened at first, and then suddenly words seemed to be appearing as if they had just been written.

"What does it say?" I asked frantically.

She began to read it aloud to the rest of us: "Mr. Bertolini, please accept this as your official invitation to the Council. To gain entry to the chamber, give this paper with the symbol to the guard located at the unmarked grave. —A.A."

"Aminoff," I said angrily.

"Where is the unmarked grave?" Kevin said, rather confused.

"I lllove gggraveyards…They are ssso peeaaccceeeful," Sal said, whispering as he always did.

"I'm sure you do, creepy guy," I said, making a scrunched face at him.

"I know where the grave is. Let's turn everything off and put everything back the way it was and then head out," I said.

"Right," everyone said as they split up to turn off whatever lights they had on and picked up whatever trace of our existence we had left behind upon our break-in. We left the house and headed back for the wood line. We made our way through the woods for about thirty minutes before arriving at the graveyard. *The sun will be coming up soon; we need to get this done quickly*, I thought.

"I need to do this alone," I said to them.

"What?" gawked Kevin.

"You literally said you would need all of us on this mission," George said angrily. "I was going to make the most beautiful explosion."

"Just this part I have to do alone. Don't you think the guard would find it strange that six people he has never seen before had an invitation to the Council's hideout?" I said.

"You have a valid point," Katie said, looking upset but accepting the fact that she had to stay hidden.

"Watch the guard," I began. "When he shows me the entrance to let me in, remember how he does it, and follow after me in about forty minutes if I'm not back," I said.

"Sounds like a plan, master," Raven said smiling.

"Please don't call me that," I said as I felt my face get warm. I began my walk toward the graveyard and toward the guard at the unmarked grave.

"Who goes there?" the guard asked, squinting at me as the sun was beginning to rise, though it was still kind of dark. I held up the paper and kept walking toward him. He looked at the paper and then at me. He began to massage his chin and then looked me in the eyes.

"You look…familiar," he said.

"I would hope so. I come here frequently, or have you forgotten?" I said to him, trying my best to impersonate the Council members. He looked at me again, up and down, and then said, "Fine."

He began to walk toward a crypt located close to the unmarked grave. He pressed one of the pillars down on the side and twisted it twice counterclockwise. I heard the sound of stone grinding as the wall slid open, allowing us to gain entry.

"Oh yeah, one more thing before you head down there," the guard said, smiling at me.

"What's that?" I asked.

"Welcome home, Andrew," he said as he quickly covered my mouth and nose with his hand. There was some sort of cloth in between the barrier. I became very dizzy, and then everything went black.

11

The Council

WHEN I CAME to, I found myself chained down, arms and legs alike, and I seemed to be lying flat on an altar of some sort. The room was dark, but there was sunlight gently creeping through a small window toward the ceiling. *I am underground,* I thought, *maybe still in the crypt, but I'm not one hundred percent sure at this point.* The way the light was coming in, it was close to noon. I remembered telling the team that they should follow me after forty minutes. That clearly hadn't happened, or I wouldn't have been in this situation right now. I wiggled my arm and leg gently to see how tight the chains were on my limbs. Too tight to slip through, it would seem. Even if I broke my thumb and tried to slip through, the clasp was too tight around my wrists. I looked around the room and noticed there was a door directly in front of me and some torches on the walls, which had not been lit. Other than that, the room was completely empty. Then I heard footsteps coming from where the door was. The door began to open slowly, and a figure came walking in, wearing black robes and a mask identical to what I had seen when I'd been dragged into the van many weeks ago. He was carrying a torch and began to walk around the room, lighting each one that was waiting on the wall for him.

"The Council," I said softly, "You are a member of the Council, aren't you?"

After I said this, he was finishing up the last torch and approached me. He stood over me where my head was and was peering down onto me. *Wait a second…*I thought. *That isn't a man…Those eyes, I know those eyes!* She winked at me but said nothing as more people in similar attire entered the room. There were only seven in total, including the woman standing over me. She moved from behind me to my left side with two others. Three of the other figures were now standing on my right, and only one stood before me.

"I had so much faith that you would die in Vorkuta," the man said.

My heart sank because I knew who this man was. He removed the mask and shed light on his face. Aminoff—I knew he was behind all of this.

"What is going on?" I asked, holding his gaze.

"It's simple," he began. "It has come to my attention that we needed to restructure our order. In order to do so, we first had to take out your father. After that, we had to get rid of you, but it seems it's a little bit harder to get rid of you, now, isn't it?" he said, glaring at me.

"You!" I yelled. "You are the one who alerted the Soviets

about the hit. You wanted me to be captured and sent to the gulag."

"Yes, it was me and that was the plan. Never in my dreams did I think you would be able to escape such a putrid place with such ease. It's rather frustrating, if you ask me," he snarled. "However, it seems that I need to get rid of you myself."

"Before you kill me, can you at least tell me why you killed my father?" I asked him.

"Restructuring. He was just a speed bump in the process. Sometimes people won't change their ways and conform with the rest when necessary," he said as he pulled a dagger from his robe that seemed to be exquisitely made. It had a golden handle and a ruby on the hilt. The blade was long, curved, and very sharp. "Farewell, Andrew," he said as he began to walk around to my left side and toward my head. He was standing directly above and began to reach out with the knife toward my neck but was stopped. The woman on the left side stopped him and was holding his wrist.

"What do you think you are doing?" Aminoff sneered, looking at her.

"You won't hurt him," she said as she twisted his arm and grabbed the knife with her other hand. The two men who were standing behind her lunged toward her. She threw a rather impressive kick, knocking one of the men directly into the other, and they both went tumbling to the ground. She had control of the knife, but Aminoff had broken free and took a couple steps back. The woman removed her mask, and not to my surprise, I was now looking at the beautiful Anya.

"It's six against one," Aminoff said. "You can't beat us."

"You shouldn't underestimate me," she said as she began to walk toward Aminoff.

He began walking around, toward the right side of the room, and stood behind the three Council members on the right.

"Take care of her, and come find me when you have finished." He walked out of the room and closed the door behind him. The two men Anya had knocked down began to get back up. The three men on my right began to walk around me and the altar, toward Anya.

"Now it's five versus one, and I have the knife. I like these odds," she said with a wicked smile. One of the men from the right lunged at her, but she dodged him and stabbed him in the neck.

"One down, four to go," she said, moving a strand of hair from her face with the back of her hand. I'd never realized how long her hair was; she always had it pulled back. Now one from the left and the right charged her at the same time, and she threw a spinning back kick on the man to the left, knocking him to the ground. The man on the right still was able to complete a successful charge and pinned her up against the wall. One of the men grabbed the knife that had fallen from Anya's hands as she was slammed against the wall. "Don't be a fool. Four versus one is still impossible, even for the best assassin," he said, gripping the knife tight.

"End it!" one of the men yelled from behind me. The man raised the knife toward Anya, and then the door suddenly slammed open.

Bang. Bang. Bang. Bang.

Each of the men had fallen to the ground, perfect shots. There was a man standing in the doorway holding a pistol.

"I'm glad I can still shoot well," said Dragutin, chuckling, as he entered the room.

"And in perfect time," Anya said, walking toward him.

"You guys know each other?" I asked, confused.

"Yes, well, we kind of just met recently, actually," she said.

"We can explain it once we get out of here," Dragutin said as he began to unshackle me from the chains. I rubbed my wrists because they were rather swollen from being clasped so tight.

"Where's the rest of my team?" I asked urgently.

"I told you, I'll explain everything once we get out of here," Dragutin said. We made our way out of the room and made a right down the hallway. We certainly were not down in that crypt I'd thought I would have been in from before.

"Where are we?" I asked.

"Shh," Anya said as she covered up my mouth.

I nodded, and she removed her hand from my face. We continued to walk quietly, corner after corner, hallway after hallway. Eventually, we made it to a room that said "Security" on the side of it. Dragutin raised his hand in a halting fashion for us to wait here. He moved to the opposite side of the door and opened it. He peered in and then opened the door the rest of the way. He entered the room and then came back out a couple seconds later.

"Come in," he said as we entered the room. There were TVs set up showing footage of what looked like a rather large compound with many rooms. Security cameras of where we were, apparently.

"It would seem Aminoff has gotten away," he said as he was pressing a button, and we saw footage rewinding on the TV. He pressed play, and it showed Aminoff escaping through a door leading outside.

"This isn't good," he said with a frown. "But for now, we will celebrate a small victory." He stood up and left the room.

"C'mon, Andrew. There's something I need to show you," he said. We left the room and made our way through the halls, and eventually we made it to a common area.

"Andrew!" I heard a yell from Katie as she jumped out of her chair. The common area was rather large and had large paintings hanging on the walls. There were bookshelves spaced evenly between each painting. There was a beautiful area rug taking up the majority of the center of the room. There were also a couple couches and chairs surrounding a large coffee table in the center. To my surprise I saw my whole team in this room and...my father!

"Dad?" I said, walking toward him.

"Yes, son, it's me," he said as he came up and gave me a hug.

"I thought I killed you!" I said, hugging him.

"I know, it was necessary for you to think so," he said. "Have a seat and I'll tell you everything." I sat down, and everyone gathered so we could all listen to what the heck was going on.

"You see, I knew Aminoff was plotting on killing me. So I managed to swap his poison he planned on dosing me with a paralysis agent. Essentially, it slowed my pulse and breathing to such a slow point that no one could really detect me being alive and would assume me dead," he said. "I knew Aminoff would want to have my body taken care of afterward, but I also knew he was too lazy to take care of it himself. I made sure that his cleaner knew prior to the incident what was going on. Luckily, he stayed true to me instead of Aminoff."

"You lucked out there," I said.

"Yes, I did. Then I couldn't return home, so I wrote a letter to the only other person I could trust in the Council," he said.

"So Dragutin is in the Council," I said, remembering our findings earlier. He was giving me a smile, standing behind the couch.

"Indeed he is. However, Amnioff wanted to take complete control over the Council and have us listen directly to him. He managed to gain the support of the other Council members except for Dragutin and I," he said.

"I understand now," I said, putting everything together.

"So we killed the rest of the Council. Are you planning on rebuilding?" I asked.

"Well, yes, we are," he said, smiling. "The Council will now consist of me, Dragutin, Katie, Kevin, Sal, George, Raven, you, and that young man you met while being held in the gulag," he said.

"You'd let someone who never went to school join our ranks and be put immediately into the Council?" I asked, astonished.

"Do you trust him?" he asked.

"With my life," I said.

"We need people we can trust right now, son. Both Dragutin and I have agreed that you all are worthy to serve with us," he said as he stood up. "We are going to war."

12

A New Allegiance

WE WERE SITTING in the room looking at each other now and waiting for what else my father had to say to us.

"Well, first things first. Now that you are all official members of the Council, you need to get the brand," Father said.

"A brand?" Kevin said with his face turning slightly pale. "That sounds…very painful."

"Ohhhh, yessss…brandddd me," Sal said as we all looked at him.

"Yeah…anyways, yes, a brand. Dragutin and I both have the brand. It does hurt, yes, but it shows you are really one of us. You can get it in any location you would like, but it is mandatory," he said with a rather serious look.

"I don't understand. Why is it mandatory?" Raven asked.

"Well, think about it like this. The pain you will feel from this brand will be unbearable. But if you ever seem to be captured, you will look back at this pain and use it to remain calm and silent. Other than that, it is also a sign of dedication to our cause," he said as he stood up. "Let's get the brand out of the way first, then we will continue our missions.

"What?" I asked. "Why wouldn't we focus on Aminoff?"

"Simple, do you want the rest of the world to think our order is failing?" my father said, looking back at me. "It's all about illusions, son. We have to keep our strong appearance. Or else the nations may decide to team up against us and wipe out our order," he said sadly.

"I see," I said. "Right, then, let's get this show on the road." I got up and followed my father as well as everyone else. We made our way back to where the room with the stone altar was.

"Wait right here," he said, as we walked back out of the room.

"I have mine on my chest," Dragutin said, smiling. He pulled his arm from his sleeve and lifted his shirt so we could see his brand. "Not going to lie to you guys, it does hurt like crazy," he said with a chuckle. My father came back with a blowtorch and a branding iron with a symbol attached to it.

"This is the sign of the Council," he said as he began to heat up the brand. "With this, you will join an elite brotherhood that has been around for centuries. The only thing that changes over time is technology. Our traditions and purpose will always remain the same." He paused for a moment, then turned his gaze toward me.

"All right, where are you going to get yours?" he asked me. I thought about this for a second and then said, "I want it the same place you got yours."

He smiled at this and said, "All righty, roll up your left

pant leg." I did as he said. "Lie facedown on the altar. George and Dragutin, you two steady his leg. I'd hate to have to do it twice."

"Right," they both said as they walked toward the altar. I lay down face-first, as instructed. I felt George and Dragutin grab hold of my leg and press firmly into the altar.

"Deep breath now," my father said as he placed the scalding brand on my left calf. I let out a grunt as it seared my flesh. He held it there for about three seconds before removing it from my leg. The smell of burnt flesh filled the room. The pain was not as bad as I had thought it would be. It felt like a giant bee sting. The flesh continued to sizzle long after the branding iron was pulled away from me.

"We have medical supplies to take care of it. We have to make sure we keep it clean. I would hate for that to get infected," my father said with a smile.

"I'd like to stay and watch the others if that's okay," I said.

"Of course," he said. So I did, and one after one, each new member of the Council received their glorious brand as a welcoming gift. When it was all said and done, we made our way to the medical room and patched ourselves up.

"Two weeks," my father said.

"What?" I asked.

"It will be two weeks before you guys can go out on missions. We have to let those heal first. This allows us to plot our next series of missions and also gather intel on Aminoff in the process," he said. We did exactly that: we took our time hanging out in the new Sanctuary, which was so much nicer than the Western Sanctuary we had been staying in. Poor Doug, we had him summoned to the island and to the new Sanctuary without him knowing he had to be branded. When he arrived, he was super excited that he was a member of the order and had been reading all the books we had in the secret room. The excitement quickly drained when we gave him his brand. After that he was a little less excited about the whole assassin life. As the end of the two weeks approached, we were all gathered in the mission room of our new home. Similar to our own Wanted Table, there was a giant pentagon-shaped table in the middle of the room with piles of papers on it.

"For our first mission, we will be getting in direct contact with Ryan Phillips," Father stated.

"The CIA director for the US?" Dragutin asked, uncertain.

"Yes," my father said.

"Why exactly would we do that? That would be unwise, I feel, as a secret order of assassins," he said, confused.

"Well, I'm glad you asked. The reason is simple: Aminoff has fled to the Soviet Union according to my contacts. Apparently, he has manipulated our own sanctuaries we have throughout the Soviet Union to believe that the rest of the Council was taken out. So now we have an opposing faction breaking off from our own order who will be loyal to Aminoff and his ideas," Father said angrily.

"And you think that he will begin to work with the Soviet government?" Dragutin said.

"Yes, I believe that we will have no choice but to align ourselves with the Americans," my father said.

"Why not just go directly to the president?" asked Raven.

"An assassin setting a meeting with a president...You do the math on that one," Vince said, laughing.

"So the CIA is our way in?" I asked.

"Indeed, so who better to send than you, Andrew. I will be sending you to meet with him at the Western Sanctuary. We are going to be giving them it as a generous donation toward our future alliance and friendship," he said. "Go ahead and get ready for your flight and meeting. You will be on your way shortly."

I left the room and heard as he was assigning other missions to my fellow Council members. Interesting, I'd never thought I would be having a diplomacy mission in my lifetime. I made my way through the many hallways of this sanctuary and followed the stairwell back to the main floor and out of the sanctuary. Who would have thought, they placed the most secret sanctuary of all right below Black Fawn Academy? I walked through the halls of the school, passing by classes being taught to the children. I had many memories passing through my mind as I continued to make my way out of the building. I made my way to the parking lot, where a driver and car were waiting for me.

"Afternoon, sir," he said to me with a half bow.

"Hey," I said to him, and he seemed rather taken aback at my laxation.

"Are we heading to the airport?" he asked as we both got into the vehicle.

"Yes, sir." The driver put the car into drive and took us on our way. It took only about twenty minutes to reach the airport. When we arrived there was a small jet waiting for me, and Doug.

"Hey, Andrew!" he said to me as I boarded the plane. "I guess I'm really just going to be the aviation guy in the order, it would seem," he said with a chuckle. "Where are we headed?" he asked.

"To the Western Sanctuary," I said. He turned around and readied the plane for takeoff. I ended up falling asleep on the flight over, because I woke up to Doug poking my face.

"You really can sleep, can't you?" he said. I gave a big stretch and stood up.

"Oh, I know," I said, wiping some drool from the side of my face. I climbed down from the plane and met another driver, who was waiting at the strip.

"Evening, sir," he said to me as I said nothing and got in the car.

"Western Sanctuary," I told him, and he tipped his hat, and we were on our way. The car ride there was very silent, but I didn't mind the sound of silence. It gave me time to think to myself about everything crazy going on. I wondered if Aminoff would form a new Council or have an authoritarian style of ruling. We pulled into the garage, and I got out. There were two very fancy black cars in the garage, but they were empty. I went to the elevator and made my descent down to my old home.

Ding.

I stepped off the elevator, and there were two men in suits standing there.

"Mr. Bertolini?" one of them said, rather serious. They were both very muscular and had tight trimmed haircuts and were very professional looking.

"Mr. Phillips is waiting for you in the common area," he said as they both moved out of my way and were staring at me.

I made my way down the hall and entered the common room, where Phillips was standing.

"Ah! Yes, you must be the one from that 'order' I've heard so much about over the years," he said, smiling. He stuck out his hand, and I gave a firm handshake. He was very tall, bald, and had no facial hair. He had blue eyes and a constant smirk on his face.

"So you want to work for us?" Phillips said.

"No, sir, not work for you but work with you," I said.

"Well, giving us this hideout was a great start. We needed a new place to move our experiments we have been doing," he said. "However, if you are so bent on working together, please tell me one of your accomplishments."

"Well, for starters, I assassinated Olaf Yahontov," I said and saw his eyes widen.

"Well then, that it is a hefty accomplishment. I've been trying to get rid of that man for years now. I heard the assassin who did that was captured, though?" he said.

"I was, and I was taken to the Vorkuta Gulag. Then luckily escaped with my life," I said. He seemed very impressed by this.

"So you are telling me you know the layout of the biggest prison the Soviets have. Maybe we can work together, then," he said, smiling. "I have one condition, though."

"Name it," I said back.

"We will allow you to conduct hits that we need taken out, and we will ally ourselves with you. But if you are ever captured, we will not come and rescue you or acknowledge our allegiance to the general public. It would look rather bad if our country realized we had our own assassin ring in our back pockets," he said with a chuckle.

"I can agree to these terms," I said as I stuck my hand out, and we gave a promising handshake.

"Splendid, well then. Let's get down to our first mission together, then, shall we?" Phillips said.

"Certainly," I said.

"Our first target we would like you to take out is a military officer by the name of Klasovich," he said with a smile.

"You want me to go back to Vorkuta?" I asked, annoyed.

"That shouldn't be a problem, seeing as you were already there before, right?" he said as the smile faded from his face. He was right, I could easily sneak back in. The only problem was I would need to be very stealthy on this mission, and the escape would have to be perfect. I would not be able to take the helicopter from a roof like last time because they probably had countermeasures in place for this.

"Fine, I think I can manage that," I said.

"Perfect!" he said with a smile back on his face. "Oh yeah, one more thing."

I looked at him, waiting for what he had to say.

"I want you to…take a doctor of mine with you. We kind of can't be tied to him anymore. But we don't think he deserves to die, because he has brilliant ideas he still needs to conduct for research," he said.

"What could you possibly need to get rid of a doctor for?" I asked, perplexed.

"Let's just say we were experimenting the effects LSD has

on—" His story was cut short as the doctor walked into the room. He seemed to be making a clanging noise as he walked.

"Hello, the name is Dr. Comer. Nice to meet you," he said with a smile. I figured out why he was clanging: the man had two fake metal legs, and he also only had one arm.

I must have been making a funny face because he said, "There was an accident with one of my experiments."

I nodded. "The name's Andrew, pleasure to meet you," I said as I shook his only hand. He was pretty short, with very low-cut hair and a decent-sized beard.

"Well then, I suppose I'll be heading out, then," I said.

"Glad we got everything worked out. It's good to have you as an official unofficial ally of the United States," Phillips said with a wink.

13

The Return to Vorkuta

DR. COMER AND I made it back to Black Fawn Academy and made our way to the hidden sanctuary beneath the school.

"I do say, I shall be a splendid asset to the team. I truly love pushing the human mind to new limits," Dr. Comer said.

"For some reason…I'm sure you and Sal will get along splendidly," I said with a chuckle.

I made my way through the halls and into the mission planning room, where we always prepped. Katie and Kevin were in there reviewing some documents on the table.

"Hey, Andrew, how'd it go?" Kevin asked.

"Who's that?" Katie said, looking at Dr. Comer.

"This is our newest member of the team. His name is Dr. Comer, and he does…psychological experiments? I think," I said.

"To be exact, I've been working on controlling people's minds with LSD," he said excitedly.

Katie and Kevin looked at him like he was a bit estranged. Meanwhile in the shadows behind us, eyes flashed with excitement, and Sal revealed himself.

"Ppplease tell me mmmmore on this," Sal said, staring eagerly at Dr. Comer.

"Of course! Say, why don't we find some place more relaxing to talk," Dr. Comer said.

"Certainly, let's ggggo to the common area," Sal said happily as they made their way out of the room. At this point Dragutin and Vincenzo walked into the room.

"Hey son, how'd it go?" Father asked me.

"Well, as you could see we have a new member…but it seems Sal has taken a liking to him. Also, Phillips will work with us, but I need to do something first as a first mission with him kind of thing," I said.

"Oh yeah? And what is it he wants you to do?" Dragutin asked.

"Well, they want me to go back to Vorkuta and kill Klasovich," I said scratching the back of my head, smiling.

"You seem more than capable of doing that. I mean, you did escape from there, didn't you?" Father said.

"That is exactly what Phillips said." I sighed.

"Anyways, I really shouldn't have any problems doing this hit. I just hope they don't recognize me on the way in," I said.

"What do you mean?" Dragutin said.

"Well, the best way for me to get into the Vorkuta is to impersonate a Soviet soldier…or become a prisoner again," I said.

"He's right, it is the better of the two options. At least as the soldier he can sneak in undetected the best he can and have a weapon and not seem suspicious. Being a prisoner would only hinder him from completing his mission," Father said.

"Right, I'll go find a uniform for you from the armory. Last time I checked, we had some old Soviet Uniforms in there," Katie said as she left the room.

"So what else will you need, Andrew?" Dragutin asked.

"I think I want this to be stealthy as possible…no bombs this time, maybe some sleeping agents if possible?" I said, looking up to Kevin.

"Certainly, would you prefer darts or needles?" Kevin asked, smiling.

"Let's go with darts just in case. That way they can be projectile or close combat if needed," I said to him, nodding.

"Cool, I'll go gather them and meet up with Katie," Kevin said and left the room as well.

"Well, I think you got this all taken care of, boy," Dragutin said and left the room. My father was still there, and he was standing there smiling. He approached me and put his hand on my shoulder.

"I'm proud of the man you have become," he said and gave me a hug.

"Thanks," I said as he let go.

"I should be prepping to leave here soon. Will you all be running missions when I'm gone?" I asked.

"Certainly, there's a pretty big mission coming up. I'll let you know how it goes when you return from Vorkuta," he said.

After that I made my way out of the room and toward the armory, where Katie and Kevin were both waiting for me. "Here everything is, Andrew," Katie said with a smile.

"Awesome, I'll go ahead and get changed and be on my way. I'd like to get this done and over with," I said.

I really didn't want to go back to Vorkuta, but it's what's best for the order, and we needed to stop Aminoff. Katie and Kevin left the room, and I changed into my uniform and placed the sleeping darts in my left cargo pocket. At that I made my way from the armory and was prepared for the journey back to the Soviet Union. I left the sanctuary and Black Fawn and made my way to the airstrip, where Doug was waiting for me.

"Man, I sure am glad I'm not you right now," Doug said with an uncertain face.

"Don't worry, I'll make it back out again alive, you can count on it," I said with a smile.

"All right, well, knowing you…You'll probably fall asleep on the way over there, so I'll wake you up when we land at the air base," he said.

Doug knew me well for our short time being together. I did indeed fall asleep and was awakened to him again poking me in the face like last time.

"Okay, okay, I'm awake," I said, getting down from the plane. I adjusted my uniform to make sure I looked prim and proper and to the Soviets' standards.

"Good luck, Andrew. I'll be waiting here with Collyn until you get back," he said as I made my way over to a vehicle that was waiting for me. The driver was standing there and looking at me.

"I need you to take me to the closest military base near Vorkuta. But don't take us on post," I said, looking at him.

He nodded as we got into the car and made our way to the base.

"Park right here," I said, as we were now currently outside of the base, slightly out of distance of the main gates to gain access to post. The security didn't seem too uptight; in fact, it looked like there were only two guards checking IDs and letting people in. *Perfect*, I thought, *this should be an easy in-and-out mission.* "Take us to the gate, and we will gain entry," I said to the driver.

We approached the gate, and I rolled down my window from the back seat.

"Identification," the soldier said.

"Well, you see, I left it on post, which is why I'm coming back. It's lying on my desk in the barracks," I said in Russian with a smile. The guard looked at me for a second and observed my uniform for any discrepancies. Then he let out a sigh.

"Fine, I'm going to remember your face though. If this happens again, I won't let you back in until your platoon sergeant comes to get you," he said with a stern face.

"Understood," I said as the gate was pulled open in front of us. The driver proceeded to drive onto post. I had the driver take us around the post until I found the motor pool.

"I'll get out here," I said to him. He stopped the vehicle, and I got out and made my way through the gates of the motor pool. *Which one should I choose?* I thought as I looked at all the vehicles and was trying to decide which one would suit me best for the entry of the gulag. I decided to go with an UAZ-3172 that was sitting toward the back of the motor pool. I noticed the door was unsecured, and I gained entry to the vehicle. I popped the bottom of the dash off and began searching for the right wires. I used my knife to cut and touch the wires needed and started up the vehicle with ease. *Right, now I can get this over with.* I drove out from the motor pool and made my way off post. I waved at the gate guard on my way out, and he just gave me a dead stare. I arrived at the gulag and parked and made my way in through the front door like I was just one of the regulars. *This place is so big, surely no one will notice I'm not one of them,* I thought. I was right: everyone thought I was just one of the guards, just like them. I needed to find an ID card to gain entry to certain levels of the gulag, I remembered from when I had killed Ivan and snatched his badge. I noticed there was a soldier talking to another soldier, and his ID card was clipped to his waist, unlike most, who had them dangling around their necks or tucked away in a pocket. I made my way toward them and bumped into them by "accident" and during the process snagged the ID off his waist and into my pocket.

"Sorry," I said as I walked away from them.

They looked at me rather oddly, but I continued my way through the many halls of the gulag. *Klasovich's office has to be close to the rooftop, I would assume, since he always had it as an emergency exit,* I thought. I made my way to the stairwell and up several floors. I opened the door with the ID I had snagged and gained entry. There were many different rooms on this floor, and they seemed to be like offices. It was quiet, uneasily quiet. I began to walk through the hallway and noticed in many of the rooms there were bodies. Soviet soldiers' bodies lying on the ground, and they seemed to have been killed with stab wounds. *This is not good.* I made my way to the last office room, which I assumed to be Klasovich's. As I entered the room, the chair behind his desk was facing away from me, but

I saw the top of the back of his head in the chair. I walked cautiously over to the chair and spun him around. Dead, just as I'd thought, but who could have possibly done this? Who else would want Klasovich dead? I felt cold sharp steel close to the right side of my neck.

"Turn around slowly," a voice said. It was a man's, but I did as he asked. The man was wearing all black and was wearing a mask as if he was going to be skiing sometime soon. He was very slender, and I definitely felt like I could beat him in a fight.

"Who are you?" I asked, looking at him.

"You are the one Aminoff warned me about," the man said.

I looked at him sternly now. *I see this is one of his new associates, it would seem.* But why on earth would he be here to kill Klasovich?

"He had a feeling that you would align yourself with the United States and make your way back here to kill Klasovich," he said. It was highly annoying how well Aminoff's intelligence was and that he's always a step ahead.

"Yes, well, it would seem he was right, but it also seems unfortunate for you," I said as I swiftly knocked his arm away from my neck and gave a strong punch to his chest, shoving him away from me.

"I'm not here to fight you. I'm just here to talk," he said.

"Make it quick, and I'll decide whether you leave here alive or not," I said to him coldly.

"I was instructed to come here and kill you by Aminoff... But I have a couple of questions first," he said.

"Spit it out already," I said angrily.

"Okay, okay, is it true that all the Council has died? And

that you staged a coup d'état and took over the Council?" he asked.

"No, Aminoff has lied to you. That's not what happened at all," I said, and then I told him everything that had happened.

"I see," he said as he lowered his knife from in front of him and stood more passively. "It would seem he has deceived many who are in the Soviet Union's sanctuaries. Not only that, but he went straight to the Soviet government and requested that they align themselves to further each other's goals," the man said.

"I…I want to help you," the man said.

"How do you propose you do that?" I asked as I lowered my fighting stance as well.

"I'd like to be your inside man. I can help you get any intelligence you need on Aminoff and can report directly to you," he said. I stood there and considered this for a moment. This would be very beneficial for us; we could easily root out Aminoff and take back control of our order and not have to have a full-on war.

"I agree, let's get out of here and discuss it further," I said to him as I looked over at Klasovich's body. *I wonder if this guy will really be helpful or if he will end up being our downfall*, I thought. *I suppose time will only tell.*

To be continued…